I0638041

Sunset
After
Midnight

SPLASH™

SUNSET AFTER MIDNIGHT is a publication of SPLASH
an imprint of J. Boylston & Company, Publishers.

Splash is a registered trademark of J. Boylston & Company,
Publishers, successor-in-interest to the General Licensing Company, Inc.

Sunset Island and *Sunset After Dark* are trademarks of
J. Boylston & Company, Publishers, successor-in-interest
to the General Licensing Company, Inc.

Habent Sua Fata Libelli

Splash
Manhanset House
Shelter Island Hts., New York 11965-0342

bricktower@aol.com • www.ibooksinc.com

All rights reserved under the International and Pan-American
Copyright Conventions. No part of this publication may be reproduced,
stored in a retrieval system, or transmitted in any form or by any means,
electronic, or otherwise, without the prior written permission of the
copyright holder.

The SPLASH colophon is a trademark of
J. Boylston & Company, Publishers.

Library of Congress Cataloging-in-Publication Data
Bennett, Cherie by Jessica Lynn.
Sunset After Midnight
p. cm.

1. Young Adult Fiction—Girls & Women.
2. Young Adult Fiction—Romance—Clean & Wholesome.
3. Young Adult Fiction—Romance—General. Fiction, I. Title.

978-1-876969-53-0, Trade Paper

Copyright © 1993 by General Licensing Company
April 2025

Sunset After Midnight

CHERIE BENNETT BY
JESSICA LYNN

SPLASH™
Habent Sua Fata Libelli

"Tony passed!" Darcy shot back.

"Now you're telling me not to believe the lie detector test?"

"Hey, Darcy, lighten up," Scott said. "I'm just doing the best job I can on this case. I mean, what do you really know about this guy?"

Darcy stood up. "I don't know. What do you know about me, Scott? Do you have a full report on me, from the FBI maybe?" she challenged.

"I don't need one on you, Darcy," Scott said. "You're not a suspect."

"Look, Scott," she said finally. "I think the problem isn't Tony, but that I'm dating Tony. So I think the best we can do right now is stay just friends."

"No," Scott said, "that's not the answer. I don't want to be just friends with you, Darcy. And if I can't have what I want, I don't want to see you. "

The SUNSET ISLAND series
by Cherie Bennett

Sunset Revenge
Sunset Sensation
Sunset Magic
Sunset Illusions
Sunset Fire
Sunset Fantasy
Sunset Passion
Sunset Love
Sunset Fling
Sunset Tears
Sunset Spirit
Sunset After Dark
Sunset After Midnight
Sunset After Hours

ONE

College. I can't believe I'm actually in college, Darcy Laken thought to herself, staring down at her new notebooks with a huge grin on her face.

She heard her father's words on the phone the night before echoing in her head: "Darcy, girl," he'd said in his faint Irish brogue, "you're the first Laken going to college. Make us proud."

I will, Dad, she promised him fervently in her head. Then she looked around the student lounge at the excited students milling about.

"Jenny!" a blond-haired girl squealed, throwing her arms around a short brunette. "God, you look fabulous! You lost a ton of weight!"

"Can you believe it?" the shorter girl laughed. "I am so totally psyched!"

Darcy smiled wistfully at them as they walked away together. Seeing them made her miss her best friend from high school, Suki, who had moved across the country. The first day of college would have been so much easier if Suki had been with her.

Darcy shrugged and tossed her long black hair back over her shoulders. *So, big deal, Laken*, she told herself. *This is hardly the scariest thing you've ever faced in your life.*

"Well, look who's here," came a fake and obnoxious voice that Darcy recognized all too well. She looked up into the bright blue eyes of Marianne Reed, her arch-enemy from high school. Standing with Marianne were three other girls, who looked Darcy over with supercilious delight.

It all came rushing back to Darcy—the years rich Marianne had taunted her for being poor and wearing clothes from the Salvation Army. And then the final blow—when Marianne had won the college athletic scholarship that Darcy had deserved to win. Darcy had needed the scholarship desperately and was devastated by the loss. At the time, she'd thought it was the only way she'd ever get to college.

"So, Darcy," Marianne began sweetly, "I'm so surprised to see you here. Did you win the lottery or something?"

"A rich uncle," Darcy murmured. Marianne Reed was the last person on earth she wanted to tell how she was able to afford college after all.

"Great," Marianne said with a grin. "Too bad he didn't pay for your clothes in high school. Wasn't he embarrassed, having his niece running around in rags?"

Darcy pushed her chair back abruptly, practically knocking Marianne over. She stood up, towering over the other girl. "Hold still, Marianne, you've got something on your nose." Darcy grabbed Marianne by the collar so the smaller girl couldn't move and then she slowly moved her hand to Marianne's face. She knew Marianne had to be thinking about the time, years ago, when Darcy had punched Marianne's lights out for making fun of her clothes at school.

Marianne cowered, her mouth gaping open. Her friends just stood around looking stunned. Finally, Darcy let go of Marianne's shirt and pushed her away. "Oh, gee, I guess it's just the way your nose is. Sorry." Darcy picked up her books and strode away from the group of girls.

"That cow was going to hit me!" Marianne was shrieking to her friends. "I swear, she was actually going to hit me!"

Darcy kept walking, but turned around for a moment. She smiled at Marianne and waved, as if she hadn't a care in the world. Then she turned back around and kept walking.

"That was great," a male voice said with a laugh.

Darcy turned to look up into a pair of deep, penetrating brown eyes. The guy was gorgeous, tall, with thick black hair and an athlete's slender torso. He leaned against a wall and smiled at Darcy. "Were you really going to deck her?"

Darcy was a little embarrassed—her temper had gotten her in trouble before—but she had to laugh anyway. "It wouldn't be the first time," she admitted.

The guy threw back his head and laughed heartily. "I love a girl who can throw a good punch. I'm Antonio Mendez," he said easily, putting out his hand. "Call me Tony."

"Darcy Laken," Darcy said, shaking his hand. "Listen, I've got to run to my first class—"

"Me, too," Tony said, falling in beside her. "Intro to Criminology." He wiggled his eyebrows in a comically sinister fashion.

"Me, too!" Darcy said with surprise.

"It's fate," Tony decided, and they chatted easily all the way to Montgomery Hall, where the class was being held.

"Ladies and gentleman, if you'll all find seats, please," the professor was saying as Tony and Darcy slipped into the room. "This is Introduction to Criminology. I'm Professor Aaron. Let's go over the required reading list. . . ."

Darcy already knew the required reading list, and her mind wandered back over how incredibly her life had changed in the past few months. Her family had never had much money, but her parents supported their five children the best they could. After her father's stroke, things got really tight. Her mom worked as a waitress, and her dad had some disability money coming in. Still, there were times when they'd even had to receive food stamps, much to Darcy's embarrassment. She'd vowed she would find a way to go to college, she'd find a great job—at what, she hadn't a clue—and she'd never be poor again. Then, when she'd lost the scholarship, Darcy thought she'd never be able to afford college. But, just when it looked hopeless, her life had changed.

While working in her uncle's ice cream parlor on Sunset Island the summer after high school graduation, she'd met Molly Mason. Pretty, vivacious, sixteen-year-old Molly was an ace on a horse, and she came in every day for ice cream with her riding friends. Molly and Darcy had recognized each other as fellow daredevils, and had quickly become fast friends.

And then something terrible happened.

Darcy had always had some kind of ESP—or as she said, "Sometimes I just know things." Sometimes in a flash of light, sometimes in a dream, a premonition would come to Darcy that would later prove valid. During the summer she'd even helped some friends solve a robbery.

So when she had the terrible dream that Molly would be in a gruesome accident, it really scared her.

And yet . . . at high school graduation, her psychic sense had told her that Marianne had a brain tumor growing in her head. Darcy had been absolutely certain, and she'd warned Marianne. But when Marianne went for tests, they all turned up negative (which gave Marianne still another reason to be hateful towards Darcy).

So although she'd called Molly to try to warn her, a part of Darcy felt stupid. She didn't completely trust this ESP thing anymore. Molly hadn't been home at the time, and so she never knew Darcy was trying to warn her. And then came the terrible car accident, which left the former "Maniac Mason" a paraplegic. Tears came to Darcy's eyes just remembering. A part of her would always feel guilty. *If only I'd tried harder to warn Molly*, she said to herself. *If only . . .*

Molly's wealthy parents had ended up hiring Darcy to live with them and be Molly's companion. They were even paying her college tuition. So now Darcy and Molly were as close as sisters, and Darcy lived in a mansion and could afford to go to college. But Molly was stuck in a wheelchair. Life just wasn't fair.

"What kind of personalities commit crimes?" Professor Aaron was asking from the front of the room.

Darcy was startled back to attention. She stared at the teacher with interest.

"Any kind," Professor Aaron intoned, answering his own question. "The most heinous crimes, however, are committed by what we call the psychopathic personalities. These are people who have no sense of right and wrong, no censor, as it were."

Tony raised his hand. "How much does environment have to do with it?" he asked.

"This is the old nature verses nurture question," the teacher said. "In other words, how much of behavior is genetic and how much is learned in reaction to environmental influences. We're learning more about this all the time. Psychologists certainly know there is a pattern where abused children grow up to be abusing adults, for example."

"Always?" a petite brunette asked from across the room.

"No, and that's the tough part," the teacher continued. "There is a statistically higher incidence, but how do we explain that some abused children do not continue the pattern and some do? The answer may lie in the brain. . . ."

Darcy took avid notes as the professor continue. She found the subject so fascinating that she didn't even notice the time passing. It seemed only moments before the class was over.

"Interesting stuff, huh?" Tony asked, getting up from his seat.

"Unbelievable," Darcy agreed.

"You have a class now?" Tony queried, walking beside Darcy towards the door.

"This is the only class I have on Mondays," Darcy said. "It's sort of a messed up schedule, but I really wanted to take this course."

"I've got a two–hour break," Tony said, holding the door for Darcy. "Want to go discuss the criminal mind?"

"Sure," Darcy agreed as they walked out into the bright sunshine. "Gorgeous day, huh?"

"Can't beat it," Tony agreed. He led the way to The Java, a tiny coffee shop just off campus.

"So, are you a psych major?" Darcy asked, as they settled into the booth.

"Yep," Tony said, scanning the menu. "How about you?"

"I'm majorless at the moment," Darcy said. "I mean, I haven't declared one because I haven't figured out what I want to do."

"You hungry?" Tony asked Darcy as the weary-looking waitress stood waiting for their order.

"No, just coffee is fine," Darcy told the waitress.

"Make it two," Tony said. "And a blueberry muffin," he added, handing the menu to the waitress. "So," he said, looking at Darcy with interest, "what made you want to take criminology?"

Darcy shrugged. "I don't know. It just intrigues me, I guess." *I am not about to tell him about the ESP stuff—at least not now*, Darcy thought. *I'll sound like some kind of weirdo.*

"It intrigues me, too," Tony agreed. "I've done some writing about it, actually, and—"

"Really?" Darcy interrupted with surprise. "Like what?"

"Magazine articles, newspaper articles, that kind of thing," Tony said.

"That's wild," Darcy said. The waitress set down the coffee and Tony's muffin. "Who do you write for?" she asked, adding milk and sugar to her coffee.

"Freelance," Tony said, buttering his muffin. "I did a lot of work for the *Washington Post*, a couple of things for *Newsday* . . . you want to try this muffin?" He broke off a piece and handed it to her.

"Mmmm, it's great," Darcy said with surprise.

"Yeah, the ole Java looks funky, but the muffins are homemade—the greatest," Tony said, sipping his coffee.

"So, tell me, how did you become a professional writer so young?" Darcy asked.

"I'm not that young," Tony said. "I'm twenty-two."

"An old guy!" Darcy teased.

"For a college freshman," Tony nodded. "I got used to traveling, I guess, and I never got around to going to college."

"Where did you travel?" Darcy asked, captivated.

"Oh, all over," Tony replied. "Turkey, Greece, you name it, I've probably been there. My mom is a British diplomat and my father's Spanish, so when I was a kid we were

15

always moving somewhere or other. I guess I got so used to it, I just kept it up when I set out on my own."

"I'm impressed," Darcy admitted.

"Good," Tony said with a laugh. "Want another muffin?"

Darcy shook her head no. "I would love to travel," she said with a sigh. "I want to go everywhere!"

"And try everything?" Tony asked in a teasing voice.

"Hey, you only live once," Darcy said with a shrug. "I'm not a sit-by-the-hearth-and-crochet kind of girl."

"Glad to hear it," Tony said, giving Darcy a great smile. "Ever try hang gliding?"

"No," Darcy admitted, "but I'd love to!"

"Ever jump from an airplane?"

"No—have you done those things?" Darcy asked eagerly.

"Sure," Tony replied. "I'll take you sometime, if you want."

"I want," Darcy said with certainty, although she remembered with a pang that she and Molly had been making skydiving plans just before the accident. Tony went on to tell her about some of his skydiving adventures. As she listened, she sipped her coffee and stared into Tony's gorgeous brown eyes. He stared back. *Whoa, this guy is unbelievable*, Darcy told herself.

"So, tell me more about you," Tony urged Darcy.

"Not much to tell," Darcy said with a shrug. "I come from this big Irish family—"

"It shows," Tony said.

"You think so?" Darcy asked, surprised. "Usually people can't tell I'm Irish because of the dark hair."

"Black hair, pale skin, violet eyes—Black Irish, right?" Tony asked. "It's killer," he added appreciatively.

Darcy smiled at the compliment. "Thanks." Just then, Darcy caught the time on her watch and was amazed that nearly two hours had passed. "I've got to run and catch a ferry over to Sunset Island," Darcy said, grabbing her purse. "I had no idea it was so late."

"Well, coincidence number two," Tony said, dropping some money on the table for the check. "I live on Sunset Island, too. Can I drive you home?"

"I thought you had another class," Darcy said.

"Art history," Tony said, making a face. "I'd love an excuse to skip it."

"I have a car. Thanks anyway," Darcy said, walking with Tony to the door of the restaurant.

"Hey, it was great meeting you," Tony said.

"See you Wednesday!" Darcy said with a grin, and took off for the parking lot.

As Darcy drove the Masons' oldest car (they had four) towards the ferry, her mind revved on in overdrive. Tony was easily the coolest, sexiest, most sophisticated guy she had ever met. *I could have the most incredible, romantic adventures with a guy like that*, she thought to herself.

Fantasies about Tony filled Darcy's head all the way back to the island. When she pulled the car off the ferry, she saw a small crowd of people, and caught a glimpse of a cute, young guy in a policeman's uniform writing down some information.

A wave of guilt hit Darcy. It was Scott, the guy she'd been dating. And here she was, lost in fantasies over some guy she had just met.

"Hey, Scott!" Darcy called as she got out of the car and headed towards him.

"Hi!" Scott said, his face lighting up at the sight of her. "How was your first day?"

"Great," Darcy replied. "What's shaking?"

"Someone swiped her purse," he said, nodding in the direction of a middle-aged couple who looked harried and distraught. "I'm trying to find witnesses."

"Good luck," Darcy told him, starting back for the car.

"I'll call you later," Scott called to her, and then immediately went back to work.

Darcy sighed and got back in the car. Scott was a great guy—cute, nice, honest, and crazy about her. Yet they were so clearly opposites—Darcy was reckless and spontaneous; Scott was serious and methodical.

"Why can't Scott be more like Tony?" she asked herself out loud when she stopped for a light. *Oh, get a grip*, she told herself. *You don't even know Tony.*

And yet, as she parked the car and headed for the spooky, formidable-looking mansion that she now called home, all she could think about was a certain pair of intense brown eyes, and a certain pair of lips asking her if she was willing to "try anything."

Darcy knew the answer was yes.

TWO

Darcy walked up the path to the Masons' house, looked at the familiar black door with the skull door knocker on it and grinned. *I've seen that thing a million times but it always cracks me up*, she thought to herself. She started to put the key in the lock, but the door swung open by itself.

Simon, the butler, stood inside.

"Greetings," he said in his usual ghoulish voice.

"Hi, Lurch," Darcy answered, smiling at him. *He loves to be called that*, she thought.

"Ah Darcy, you've made my day," Simon responded. "My parents should have given me that name."

Darcy laughed, and put most of her books down on the floor next to the telephone stand.

"Molly around?" Darcy asked.

"Upstairs with Judith-the-tutor," Simon answered, smoothing out a wrinkle in his jet-black suit, "looking like she'd rather be dead than doing homework."

"How lovely!" Darcy answered matter-of-factly. She and Simon cracked up. "Excuse me," Darcy continued, as she turned and bounded up the stairs.

Darcy reached the door to Molly's room and looked inside. There, Molly and her tutor had their heads bent over what looked like a geometry book. Darcy watched as Molly frowned at something Judith was explaining to her. Finally, Molly looked up and noticed Darcy standing there.

"Hiya," she said unenthusiastically. "Could you please get Judith here to leave?" Then Molly grinned slightly. "I think geometry is only slightly more fun than getting my tongue nailed to a board."

"Come on, it's not that bad," Judith said to her, pushing her own curly dark hair away from her eyes. Then she looked at Darcy. "How you doing?"

"Better than that hockey team on your sweatshirt did last year," Darcy replied, noticing Judith's New York Rangers sweatshirt.

"School okay?" Molly asked, shifting in her wheelchair.

"Pretty good," Darcy said, noncommittally. "If it's all right, I'll just sit over there on the couch and read—you two keep going."

Molly groaned. "I thought you came here to save me."

Darcy grinned. "There's no getting saved from geometry." She walked over to the couch and plopped herself down, opening the criminology book she'd carried in. Molly and Judith went back to work.

As Darcy looked at the two of them, she wondered for the thousandth time since she started to work for the Masons what it was like to be paralyzed. *Molly shouldn't be in a wheelchair! Her friends used to called her Maniac Mason because she was totally fearless. But if it weren't for Molly, I wouldn't even be able to go to college. Her parents are paying my tuition!* Darcy sighed and forced herself to start reading.

"Darcy!" Molly's voice cut through Darcy's concentration.

"Huh?"

"We're done, I'm free," Molly said. Judith stood up and started gathering her things to leave. But before she left, she gave Molly her homework assignment for the next day.

"Oh God, she's going to make this just as gross as school," Molly said, grimacing.

"Goal of my life," Judith said mock-primly. They all laughed. "Good luck with college, Darcy—I'll find my own way out." Darcy watched as Judith made her way out the door.

"So?" Molly asked.

"So what?" Darcy responded.

"College," Molly prompted her. "First day. Remember? How was it?"

"Class was okay," Darcy said, fiddling with her crim book. "And I met the hunk of the year."

Molly rolled her wheelchair closer to Darcy. "Is that so?" she asked. "Do I know this babeasaurus?"

"I don't think so," Darcy said matter-of-factly, "though he said he lives on the island now. Let me tell you—this guy is drop-dead gorgeous."

"Does he have a name?" Molly queried.

"Antonio Mendez. Tony, actually. His father is from Spain," Darcy said, getting an uncharacteristic faraway look in her eyes. "He's got lots of money."

"Did he ask you out?" Molly asked, rolling her wheelchair even closer.

"Nope," Darcy answered. "But we talked about doing stuff together."

"Ask him out," Molly said directly. Darcy smiled.

"I don't know, Molly," she said, "he's pretty different from me."

"Might be a nice change for him," Molly said, "hanging out with a lowlife like you instead of hopping on his Lear jet for the weekend." Darcy laughed. Just then, a loud, lugubrious bell sounded—dinner time.

Molly's parents were already sitting at the table when Darcy and Molly got off the small elevator that had been installed after Molly's accident. They made their way into the dining room. Darcy saw that Molly's mother, Caroline, was dressed in her typical Addams Family style—long, flowing black dress with pointy sleeves, and blood-red fingernails. And Gomez—his real name was Edward but he insisted everyone call him Gomez— had on black silk pajamas and his hair was parted in the middle.

"You guys look great," Darcy said, sitting down to the table. *I must be getting used to this*, she thought to herself. *If I ever start dressing like that please commit me to the closest asylum.*

"Thanks Darcy," Gomez said, passing Darcy some salad dressing in a bowl that looked like a raven.

"Darcy met a gorgeous guy at school today," Molly said, as if she were talking about the weather.

"That so?" Gomez asked, taking a bite of salad. "Can't be as beautiful as my ghostly princess," he continued, motioning to Caroline.

Caroline blushed red against the white of her pancake makeup. "Let Darcy tell us about him," she said.

Darcy took a sip of water, and described how the day had gone.

"So," Molly said, chewing on a hunk of bread, "I told Darcy that she needs to make the first move—ask him out."

"Capital idea," Gomez said. "That always flatters men."

"Tony doesn't strike me as the kind of guy who gets flattered easily," Darcy replied.

"Nonsense," Caroline said, shaking her long black hair from side to side. "Before our first date, I sent Gomez a dead gerbil as a token of my esteem. Now look at us!"

Darcy's jaw dropped open for a moment, then she quickly shut it.

"You should ask him to see this new play in Portland called *Honky Tonk Angels*," Gomez said. "It was written by a friend of ours."

"That's right," Molly piped in. "I read about it in the *Press-Herald*."

"And the good thing is," Caroline added, "we've got free house seats. So there's really no excuse."

Darcy look at each of them in turn, shook her head, and then slowly smiled.

"I don't have much choice, do I?" Darcy asked. They all shook their heads at her.

"Okay. I don't want to wake up in the middle of the night with a vampire at my throat. I'll do it."

* * *

Four days later, Darcy was in her room putting on the finishing touches of her makeup when the doorbell sounded. It was the night of *Honky Tonk Angels* and Tony was supposed to pick her up at six o'clock. She looked quickly at her watch. Five-thirty. *That's weird*, Darcy thought, *he doesn't strike me as the kind of guy who'd be early for a date.*

"Darcy!" Molly's voice rang out from downstairs. "You've got company."

Darcy wiped a bit of blush from her cheek and then went downstairs to see who it was. Standing in a Sunset Island Police Department uniform was Scott.

Darcy looked at him askance. *Great timing*, she thought. *I'm wearing a new outfit and I'm-going-out makeup.*

Scott looked her over closely. "You look great," he said noncommittally.

"I'm going to a play in Portland," Darcy answered, without mentioning Tony.

Scott smiled, but Darcy could see he was trying to figure out what was going on. "Well, it sounds like you've got plans," he said finally. "I was going to see if you were up for four-wheeling on the beach tonight."

Now, that also sounds like fun, Darcy thought.

"Sorry," Darcy answered. "How about later in the week?"

"You got it," Scott said. "I'm on duty until eight o'clock every night this week. After that?" Darcy nodded. "Okay, I'm outta here."

Darcy watched him leave and get into his patrol car. *He's nice*, Darcy thought. *Really nice.* But somehow that thought had a hollow ring to it.

At a few minutes after six, the doorbell sounded again. Darcy tried to get the door before Simon, but she was too late.

"Wow, what an intro!" Darcy heard Tony say as he stared up at Simon. "Is it Halloween already?"

"Whom are you here to see?" Simon asked him ominously. "What business do you have here?"

Darcy came to Tony's rescue. "It's okay Simon," she said. "He's my date."

"He should learn some manners," Simon growled. He turned quickly and went to his quarters. Darcy and Tony looked at each other and laughed.

"Follow me," Darcy said, "and let me introduce you to Molly."

"Okay," Tony said.

Molly was in the family room. Darcy led Tony in. And she could see Molly's reaction when she looked at Tony for the first time. *Obviously, she agrees with my description of him,* Darcy thought. *She's blushing!*

"Hi Molly," Tony said easily.

He didn't even blink when he saw that she's in a wheelchair, Darcy thought. *What a cool guy!*

Molly grinned. "Nice to meet you," she said.

"Uh, no offense," Tony said, "but are your parents heavily into devil worship or something?" He indicated the odd skeleton wallpaper and the vase of dead flowers on the mantel.

Molly and Darcy laughed. "Something like that," Molly admitted. "My parents write scripts for horror movies. Did you see *AxMurder, Incorporated?*"

Tony nodded. It had been on a late-night cable broadcast the week before, during "Shock Movie Week."

"They wrote it!" Molly said proudly. "We've got the axes downstairs to prove it!" They all cracked up. Tony went over to look at some photos that were on the mantelpiece. He picked up one and looked at it with interest.

"You've got your own horse?" he said, looking at Molly with his piercing green eyes.

"Yeah," Molly answered, her expression clouding.

"Where's he board?" Tony asked.

"Sunset Stables," Molly answered. "Obviously, I can't ride him anymore." Her face fell as she looked down at her lifeless legs.

"Maybe so, maybe not," Tony answered matter-of-factly. "Fact is, I work at Foxfire Stables and we've got a riding program for the disabled." Molly shrugged. *Foxfire is the new stable out on Shore Road*, Darcy remembered.

"I mean, you know what you're doing on a horse, right?" Tony asked.

Molly shrugged again.

"Just come out to see it," Tony urged her. "No pressure. I even room there, so you can almost always find me."

"Okay, okay," Molly said finally. "You guys better get going. You'll miss the curtain." Darcy looked at her watch. Molly was right. They said their good-byes and walked outside. Darcy was surprised to see a motorcycle in front of the house.

"Nice girl, tough break," Tony said, as he handed Darcy a helmet.

"She was in a car accident," Darcy explained. "I've been trying to get her just to go out and see her horse," Darcy said, climbing on behind Tony. He took off, and Darcy held on to the back of the seat, enjoying the feel of the wind against her body, enjoying the fact that Tony was the person driving the bike.

The show was at a big theater on Congress Street in Portland. It was about four sisters who were trying to make it to the Grand Ol' Opry in Nashville. It was both hilarious and deeply moving. There were even songs written by country star Garth Brooks. Near the end, Darcy felt Tony take her hand and gently stroke the tips of her fingers.

After the curtain calls, they walked out to Tony's bike.

"Hungry?" Tony asked her. Darcy nodded.

"How about Chinese?" Tony suggested.

"Sure, I love Chinese," Darcy said easily. In the house where she grew up, her mother and father were fond of plain Irish cooking. Darcy, somehow, had developed a taste for the exotic.

Tony drove to a cute place called Cathay Manor on Front Street. Inside, he led the way to a booth with padded seats. Darcy noticed little lanterns hanging from the ceiling and soft music piped over the sound system. They ordered and then sat together, sipping black tea.

"So," Tony said, "tell me how you came to live at the Bates Motel." Darcy laughed at the reference to Hitchcock's *Psycho*.

She told Tony the story of how she and Molly had met and about the strange events that led her to become Molly's companion.

"So the weird thing is," she finished, "I had that dream and it turned out to come true."

Tony shook his head sadly. "Maybe you weren't supposed to stop it," he said.

Darcy felt her throat tighten. "I can't accept that. Look at her. Do you think she was supposed to be in a wheelchair! Do you think she deserves that?"

Tony shook his head sadly again. "I don't know," he said quietly. "But I do know that you've got a gift not a lot of people have."

"You mean my ESP?" Darcy asked.

"Yup," Tony said, taking a sip of tea. "My mother's kind of psychic, you know."

"Really?" Darcy asked. The waitress arrived with their food—two eggrolls, an order of shrimp chow mein, and something called Special Cathay Crispy Pork that Tony assured Darcy was the specialty of the house.

"Yeah," Tony replied, serving Darcy before he served himself. "Whenever I skipped doing my homework in junior high school, she always seemed to know." They laughed together.

"What was it like growing up?" Darcy asked him. "Was it fun traveling around all the time?"

"Not so much," Tony said earnestly. "Not many friends. We moved too much. I think a kid needs friends more than he needs to see the world."

Gee, I'd love to see the world, Darcy thought to herself. *And I've always been able to entertain myself.*

"Wasn't it great living in Washington?" Darcy prompted him.

"Sometimes," Tony said, "and sometimes it was a real drag. I mean, having to listen to all those politicians all the time . . ." Darcy laughed.

"Must be more exciting for you than Sunset Island," Darcy said.

"The best thing about Sunset Island," Tony said softly, "is the person sitting across the table from me."

A wave of excitement shot through Darcy. *This guy really likes me*, she thought. *Well, that's cool. I really like him, too.*

And then another wave shot through her. One that she didn't expect. One that was full of fear and fright and foreboding. And it passed just as fast as it came.

Tony looked closely at her. "Are you okay?" he asked. "You look a little pale."

Darcy shook her head. *Now what was that all about?* she asked herself. "No, I'm fine," she replied.

"Must be MSG in the food," Tony said. "It'll do that."

Darcy nodded. *Must be*, she thought to herself. But then she realized she'd never before had that kind of reaction.

Not a single time before. *Well, that doesn't mean there can't be a first time*, she thought.

She turned her full attention back to the incredibly handsome, worldly guy sitting across from her and smiled to herself.

This, Darcy said to herself, *is only the beginning.*

THREE

"Is it love or an extreme case of goo-goo eyes?" asked Molly when Darcy came into her room after her date with Tony.

"Whatever it is, I don't think I've felt this before," said Darcy, sitting on the edge of her friend's bed. "We talked and talked and talked. Look at the time! It's after midnight. It was fabulous."

"What about Scott?" asked Molly.

"Scott seems more like a friend," Darcy said with a sigh. Tony had walked her to the Masons' front door and then kissed her good night, and Darcy remembered the feel of Tony's arms around her. She had basically forgotten about that weird flash she'd gotten in the restaurant—the flash that was probably nothing.

Molly shook her head. "I'm sure Scott wouldn't be happy to hear that."

"It's just that Scott is not exciting in the same way Tony is," said Darcy.

"Gotcha. Tony's done everything and he doesn't act smart about it. Is that it?"

"Yeah, that's it. He's just so natural about everything and he's so mature. . . ." Darcy's voice trailed off.

Molly smiled wistfully and picked at her bedspread. It was a gigantic quilt print of the *King Kong* movie poster.

"I'm so happy for you, Darcy," Molly said finally. "I mean, he really is gorgeous."

"Nice, too," Darcy added. *Add a great kisser*, she thought to herself. *Major league all-star kisser.*

"Too bad no one like Tony is going to come along for me," Molly laughed bitterly.

"Why not?" Darcy asked optimistically. "It's not impossible to fall in love," insisted Darcy. *I know what Molly's thinking—if she could walk, it would be different.*

"Cut the crap, Darcy. Who's going to love me like this?" She slapped her lifeless legs emphatically.

Darcy grimaced. *She has a point*, Darcy thought to herself. *It's going to take an amazing guy to see beyond her wheelchair.*

"Well, what about last summer at Colby?" Darcy asked.

"What about it?" Molly shot back.

"Remember sitting on the front lawn of the library and that guy walking by, and—"

"Pity," Molly said, "pure pity."

"It was not!" Darcy said, looking at Molly closely. "He was giving you The Look. And what about Howie Lawrence?"

Molly looked away. "Please," she said grimly. "Tony makes Howie Lawrence look like dogmeat." In spite of herself, Darcy laughed. Finally, Molly did too.

Darcy changed the subject and asked Molly about whether she'd decided to maybe get back on her horse. Molly's attitude soured again.

"No way. I'm not getting on a horse as a total crip," declared Molly hotly. "Forget it."

"But—"

"No buts, Darcy."

"It'll be fun, Molly—"

"Whatever fun I have isn't going to be as great as it was and we both know it," Molly stated flatly. "Case closed."

Darcy sighed quietly. *Well, I can't really blame her*, she thought. *If it were me in the wheelchair I'd probably be even more bitter than she is.*

"Okay, you got it," Darcy said. "But let me know when you're ready. Okay?" Molly nodded.

"Now, I've got to get to bed," Darcy said. She waved good night and went to her room, feeling a rush of compassion for her friend.

Darcy undressed and put on an oversized Boston Red Sox T-shirt, then climbed under the multi-colored quilt that covered the oak canopy bed. She loved her room. When she had first moved in, she couldn't believe the privacy and space. At her parents' house she'd had to share a bedroom with her two sisters, Patsi and Lilly.

That seems like years ago, Darcy thought, as she lay quietly. *So much has happened. And now I'm in college, with a gorgeous guy falling in love with me!*

She switched off the halogen reading lamp by her bed and let herself drift off to sleep.

Two hours later, she snapped awake. Cold sweat covered her. *What was I dreaming about?* She strained to remember. *Something awful.* She reached under her bed for the pad and pen she kept there, and began to write.

In Italy. Spain? On a gondola with Tony. Floating down some river. Big buildings on both sides. Someone sings. A picnic lunch in the mountains. The Alps? Snow on the mountain tops. No clouds. Tony near me. He moves to kiss me. I close my eyes. I feel his lips. They're ice! I open

*my eyes. I've turned to ice! I look at Tony—his whole head
is a skull.*

Darcy put down her pen. The sweat dried on her brow.
I must just be feeling guilty about Scott, she thought to herself.

But as she drifted off to sleep again, some small part of
her was afraid that her dream meant more—much more—
than she was willing to admit.

FOUR

Scott pressed his finger against the cleft in his chin as he stared at the Scrabble board.

"Time's up!" declared Darcy, looking at her watch. She sat next to Scott at a round table in the family room.

"Since when are we timing this game?" Scott asked.

"Since Darcy has no patience," Molly quipped.

"Read it and weep," Scott said, adding an "ed" to the word "hoard" that was already on the board.

"How do you always manage to find the double word scores?" Darcy asked, writing down Scott's score.

"God, have I got crummy letters," Molly sighed, laying down the word "fool" off an available "F" that was already on the board.

Scott nudged Darcy, who was staring intently at her letters. "Your turn."

"I know," she said absently, rearranging her seven letters and suddenly seeing that they spelled "Antonio."

"How romantic!" Darcy said spontaneously, realizing too late that she'd spoken out loud.

"What?" asked Scott.

"Oh, nothing," said Darcy, and quickly picked up a few letters to add to the board. Then she picked new letters and stared at them, guilt overwhelming her. *I should tell Scott I'm seeing another guy*, she told herself. *I'm acting like an idiot and*

I'm being totally unfair. But when she looked over at Scott's face, she found she just couldn't bring herself to tell him the truth. Darcy felt his gaze on her and met his blue eyes. He seemed to be asking a question without saying anything.

Does he know?

The rest of the game passed quickly, Darcy winning by a landslide.

"See, that's what I hate about Scrabble," Molly groused. "It's all in what kind of letters you get!"

"Ha, you just hate to lose at anything," Darcy told her, getting up. "You guys want some hot chocolate?"

"Sounds good," Scott said, following Darcy into the kitchen.

"Darcy, is something wrong?" he asked in a low voice.

"Wrong? No," she replied, but she felt as though she was lying by not saying anything. *How can I tell him?*

He stood behind her as she stirred the chocolate mix into the milk.

"The reason I asked is because the other night you were going out, and . . ." He stopped, searching her face for an answer.

"The Masons got me tickets to see a play," Darcy explained.

"Tickets, like plural?" Scott pressed.

"I went with a friend," Darcy said in a low voice.

"How close a friend?" Scott asked.

"I don't know yet," Darcy replied, her voice barely a whisper.

Scott stared at the floor. He was too polite to really interrogate her. Finally, he stood up and pushed his blond hair off his face. "Look, I gotta go."

"No, don't!" Darcy said quickly. "Stay and hang out with us—"

"Somehow, Darcy, I'm not in the mood anymore," Scott replied. He kissed Darcy on the cheek, said good–bye to Molly and headed out the front door. Darcy felt a chill after he was gone and wished she could pull him back and make things okay.

"What made him leave so fast?" Molly asked

"I'll tell you upstairs," Darcy said with a sigh. Molly wheeled herself into the small elevator and Darcy carried the two cups of hot chocolate up the stairs to Molly's room.

"So?" Molly asked, sipping her hot chocolate.

"So, I have to tell him about Tony, and I keep putting it off," Darcy said. "Scott's not stupid; he knows something is up."

"He's really crazy about you, you know," Molly pointed out.

"I know," Darcy agreed. "I really like him, too. It's just that—"

"He doesn't make you breathless," Molly interrupted.

"Exactly!" Darcy exclaimed. Then she winced. "God, I sound like the kind of girl neither one of us can stand."

"I forgive you," Molly said amiably. "But listen. You're right. Scott is a great guy and you really do have to tell him the truth."

"I know," Darcy agreed. "I'm supposed to be this incredibly honest person—at least that's how I think of myself. So why is it so hard to be honest about this?"

"I wouldn't know," Molly said. "I've never had two incredibly hot guys vying for my attention."

"Well, when you do you'll know how I feel," Darcy said, finishing her hot chocolate.

"Fat chance," Molly said with a snort.

Darcy turned away from Molly and put the two cups on the nightstand. "Hey, I've been thinking about the new stables," she said, eager to change the subject.

"Oh no, here she goes. The relentless codependent friend of the invalid," quipped Molly, rolling her eyes.

"You aren't an invalid," Darcy pointed out. "I've been thinking that Foxfire Stables would be a great place to keep Ebony."

Molly's eyes lit up for a moment and then she stared down at her quilt. "I don't know."

"You haven't seen Ebony since before the accident, have you?" Darcy pressed.

"You know I haven't," Molly answered in a small, hushed voice.

Darcy had thought it all out: one reason Molly might not want to visit her horse was because she might run into her old friends at Sunset Stables where he was boarded.

After the accident, Molly's friends had called and tried to visit, but she had refused to see them. Instead, Molly had grown closer to Darcy, maybe because they shared no past. Darcy didn't know. But one thing she knew for sure: Molly loved her horse and would probably want to see him again—if her old friends weren't around.

"Don't you miss him?" Darcy asked gently.

"Of course I miss him," Molly snapped, tears springing to her eyes. She wiped them away with the back of her hand. "But I don't want to think about that."

"He probably misses you, too," Darcy said.

"Maybe," said Molly reluctantly. "But I can't stand the thought of seeing him when I can't ride him!"

"Is it really better not to see Ebony at all?" Darcy asked her friend.

Molly was silent for a moment. Then she finally looked at Darcy. "You are a pain in the butt. You know that?"

Darcy just smiled and shrugged.

"Okay, let's go visit Ebony tomorrow."

"Okay," Darcy agreed nonchalantly. But when she turned her back, she closed her eyes and said a quick, silent prayer of thanks.

"There's Tony," said Molly, waving.

Darcy looked around. Foxfire Stables had numerous paddocks and a big barn, and behind a grove of trees was a beautiful, 18th–century farmhouse where she guessed the owners lived.

Tony strode toward Darcy and Molly from the barn area, leading a chestnut horse. Darcy thought Tony looked great dressed in jeans and cowboy boots. He gave her a casual hug and grinned at Molly.

"Don't I get a hug, too?" she asked.

'You got it." He handed the lead rope to Darcy and bent down to hug Molly, who laughed in his ear.

Darcy clutched the lead rope and stared at the horse in fear. *It's nuts—horses are the only thing I'm afraid of,* she said to herself. *I have to get over this!* The horse snorted and nodded his head. Darcy stayed as far from the animal as possible.

"I have to tell you, it's hilarious seeing you afraid of a little old horse," Molly said, laughing at Darcy.

"Yeah, I'm just doing it for your amusement," Darcy said, handing the lead rope to Tony as quickly as she could.

"Let me guess—you don't spend much time around horses," said Tony with a grin.

"Bingo," said Darcy. "They are one of the few things that scare me."

"Maybe we can cure you," he suggested, slipping an arm around her shoulders.

"I doubt it," Darcy said honestly.

"We'll see," Tony said. "Come on, I want you two to meet a friend of mine."

Darcy pushed Molly's chair and the three of them headed for an outdoor arena where a cute, young guy in a wheelchair was instructing a child on a horse.

"That's right. Keep Amigo guided between the reins. Keep him going straight and don't let him move away from the fence," said the young man. His russet hair shone in the bright sunlight. He wore sunglasses, jeans, and a denim workshirt. His lean face was handsome and tanned, and he had a muscular build.

"Hey, Kenny!"

The young man turned and nodded at Tony. "Yo, Tony, how're ya doing?"

"Okay. When you're done I've got people for you to meet."

"What is this, introduce the crips time?" Molly asked.

"Molly!" Darcy exclaimed, surprised at the bitterness in her friend's voice. Lately Molly's acid comments had seemed to be lessening.

"Gee, sorry if I offended you," Molly said sarcastically.

Darcy bit her lip. Molly was right. She was perfectly entitled to her own feelings.

"So, what happened to him?" asked Molly bluntly. She stared at Kenny, her fingers gripping the handles of her wheelchair. She watched his gestures as he taught the young rider.

"Kenny's the 'hippotherapy' riding instructor," explained Tony. "He used to ride champion jumpers, but he had a bad fall and injured a vertebra in his back. It paralyzed him, but he was determined to get back on a horse. He got involved in a pilot riding program for paraplegics in Portland, and then he started one here," Tony explained. "This is his family's farm."

"Why did he do that?" asked Molly.

"Maybe it makes him feel good, Molly," said Darcy gently, resting her hand on Molly's shoulder.

"That's not what I meant," Molly said. "That guy can't feel anything from the waist down, and that's how you ride a horse—from the waist down."

"There's also holding the reins, feeling the motion of the horse underneath you—the rest of your body can do that, too," Tony explained. "Anyway, Kenny's a physical therapy major at the University of Maine. He knows what he's doing."

Kenny called out, "Good work!" and easily wheeled himself toward Tony, Darcy and Molly. At that moment a very thin young woman with lank, dirty-blond hair walked into the arena and led the rider and horse out toward the barn.

"Kenny, I want you to meet Molly Mason and Darcy Laken," said Tony. "Ladies, this is Kenny Streep."

Kenny grinned at Molly and Darcy, but his hazel eyes rested on Molly. "Good to meet you. Hey, we'd better watch we don't get our spokes stuck together."

"Very funny," said Molly.

"No, I'm serious!" Kenny protested, laughing heartily. "Sometimes when we have wheelchair races out here it happens," he said. He propped his sunglasses on top of his head, and Darcy saw the amusement playing in his eyes. "I'm teasing you," he added.

"No kidding," Molly said drolly.

"Let me introduce you to my assistant," Kenny told them. "Hey, Ina, come on over here!" he called to the thin, blond-haired girl. She hesitated and then walked over to the group.

"Hi," she said in a barely audible whisper after Kenny had introduced everyone. She clutched the horse's mane in her fist and looked at Darcy with frightened eyes.

"Do you go to school near here, Ina?" Darcy asked kindly.

Ina shook her head, staring at the ground. She pulled one lank strand of hair behind her ear. "I have to go," she finally whispered, and headed back to the horses.

"What's wrong with her?" Molly asked.

"That's Ina, nutty as they come. But she sure loves horses," said Kenny, shaking his head. "Ina can sweet talk a horse into doing somersaults."

"I don't think anyone would want a horse to do somersaults," Molly said evenly, clearly not making any effort to be pleasant to Kenny.

"You're right—especially not while you're on his back." Kenny said with a laugh, obviously unperturbed by Molly's nastiness.

Molly finally gave Kenny a grudging smile. "Let's talk horses," she told him. "I'm thinking about boarding my horse here."

As Molly and Kenny talked, Darcy and Tony strolled behind the barn and along a dirt path that led into the woods. Up ahead, they saw a clearing with a bonfire.

"One of the neighbors is burning fallen leaves," said Tony absently.

"Look!" whispered Darcy, pointing at Ina, who stood behind a tree with a horse, staring in a trance at the bonfire. Ina noticed them and hid something behind her back, but from the wisp of smoke that was left, Darcy guessed she had been smoking a cigarette.

"Kenny said she was weird and he's right," said Tony. "But I don't think she'd hurt a flea."

"I hope not," Darcy said, lacing her arm around Tony's waist.

Tony and Darcy talked easily as they strolled around, finally ending up back at the stables.

"Listen, I'm going to run in and get some money from petty cash—I need to pick up some horse treats for the new mare."

"Horse treats?" Darcy laughed. "What is a horse treat?"

"It's a candy bar for horses," Tony said. "Really hideous stuff."

Tony disappeared into the house, and Darcy walked over to Kenny and Molly.

"So, think about it and let me know," Kenny was saying. "I've got to get back to work. I'll catch you later." His powerful arms wheeled him towards the stable.

"So, how do you like it here?" Darcy asked Molly.

Molly shrugged, feigning disinterest. She watched Kenny stop to talk with a student. "It's okay."

"Kenny's cute," Darcy said, looking over at him.

"He's a crip, just like me," Molly said.

"Okay," Darcy agreed. "But that doesn't mean he isn't cute."

"Really?" Molly asked, staring hard at Darcy. "Would you go out with him?"

Darcy was taken aback for a moment. It was a question she'd never really thought about before. She searched her heart for the truth, and not just what she thought she should say. "Yeah, I would, if I liked him," Darcy finally said. "I'm not saying it wouldn't take some adjustment—"

"Some adjustment?" Molly echoed. "What does that mean?"

"In my thinking, I guess," Darcy said, struggling to sort out her own feelings.

"Pretty vague, aren't you?" Molly asked sadly.

"Honestly, Mol, I never thought about it before," Darcy said simply. "I know you don't want me to hand you a bunch of platitudes."

"True," Molly said. "But it ticks me off—Tony brought me here because he thought Kenny and I should like each other, just because we're both stuck in wheelchairs. That's pretty lame, don't you think?"

Depression seemed to prevail around Molly, weighing down on both of them. Although Darcy didn't agree with Molly, it seemed to her that Molly and Kenny had much more in common than a wheelchair. But she knew that she couldn't argue with Molly once she got into one of these moods, so she left it alone.

She saw Tony approaching from the house. His expression was dark and troubled.

"I guess I won't be running any errands," he said in frustration, squinting off in the distance. "Someone's stolen money from our petty cash box."

"Maybe you just misplaced it or something," Darcy suggested.

"It's the third time this month that it's been gone," Tony said irritably. "What a pain!"

"Hey, I'll spring for the horse candy," Darcy said easily.

"You?" Tony asked with mock surprise. "Doing something nice for a horse?"

"Ulterior motives," Darcy laughed. "I'm hoping if I bribe her she'll be nice to me.

Tony smiled at Darcy and put his arms around her. *Sheer bliss,* she sighed, closing her eyes for a moment. When she opened them again, Molly was still staring after Kenny, her eyes looking sad, wistful and hopeful, all at the same time.

FIVE

"Now that you've seen the place, what do you think about moving Ebony?" asked Darcy as they drove home from the stables.

Molly stared out the window at the ocean breakers along Shore Road.

"I don't know," Molly replied. "Why would I want to board my horse in a place where someone's stealing money?"

"Dumb excuse," Darcy said bluntly. "Twelve dollars in petty cash is hardly grand larceny."

"Well, I don't want anything to happen to Ebony," Molly said.

"I don't think anything's going to happen to him there," Darcy replied, keeping her eye on the road. "Tony will watch out for him."

"That's true," Molly said. "I guess it's okay. It's a cool place and better than Sunset in a lot of ways," said Molly thoughtfully.

"Good, then when we get home we'll call—"

"But I'm not going to ride him."

Darcy turned into the Masons' driveway. "That's okay. At least you'll know he's in good hands."

When Molly called Tony to tell him that she was ready to move Ebony, Tony agreed to trailer Ebony from Sunset

Stables over to Foxfire. The next day, Darcy and Molly were ready and waiting when he arrived at the Masons' in a pickup truck with the horse trailer.

Tony stepped out of the truck and walked over to Darcy. He slipped an arm around her shoulders. "Ready to go get a horse?" he said grinning.

"Not a horse," Molly corrected. "My horse. Look, maybe you'll want to ride him for me, Tony."

"That'd be nice. Sort of a birthday present to myself," Tony said, helping Molly into the pickup truck.

"Your birthday's coming up?" Darcy asked climbing into the pickup.

"Yeah, in a couple of weeks," he told her.

Well, that's interesting, she thought. *What can I do to surprise him?*

"You don't have to wait for your birthday to ride him," said Molly, as Tony pulled out of the Masons' driveway.

"Then I won't," said Tony.

After a short drive, Tony pulled into Sunset Stables. Darcy saw Molly's expression darken as she watched two girls riding in the arena.

"I'll stay in the truck," she said.

"Why?" asked Darcy.

"Jenny and Rowena," Molly answered. "And there's nothing you can do or say that's going to make me get out of this truck. I don't want them to see me, and I sure don't want to see them!" Darcy remonstrated with her for a bit, but finally she and Tony left Molly to get Ebony and bring him to the trailer.

Darcy and Tony went up to the main house to find Mr. Berenson, the stable owner. He had Ebony and all his tack ready.

"Nice horse. We're gonna miss him," Mr. Berenson said as they walked to the barn area.

Ebony stood in a paddock on the far side of the barn and looked up inquisitively when he saw them coming.

"Want to help me catch him?" asked Tony.

"No thanks," said Darcy. *He's huge!* she thought.

Fearlessly, Tony opened the paddock gate and walked straight up to the horse. Ebony sniffed Tony to see if he was okay, dipped his nose into the halter and allowed himself to be led out of the paddock. Back at the trailer he balked a little, but Tony spoke to him softly, saying, "Easy, easy now. It's okay, we're taking you to a new home, Ebony."

By this time, Jenny and Rowena had noticed the trailer and started towards it to take a look. Darcy pretended not to see them and opened the truck door to sit next to Molly.

"Uh oh, look who's coming," said Molly. "I'm not here; I'm really not here."

"I think it's too late for that. You've been scoped," said Darcy. She was right.

Jenny and Rowena rode up right next to the pickup truck and stared inside at Molly.

"Molly Mason, is that really you?" cried Jenny. "We haven't seen you in such a long time!"

"I know," said Molly darkly. "That's the way I wanted it."

"C'mon Maniac," said Rowena, "we're still your friends."

"Which is why you're constantly visiting me, right?" Molly snapped.

Jenny and Rowena were silent for a moment. Finally Jenny spoke. "What are you doing with your horse?"

"Obviously I'm moving him," Molly said unpleasantly.

"Okay," said Jenny, her tone now equally unpleasant. "Well, if you ever decide to sell him, give me a call. It was nice to see you, Molly. You too, Darcy."

Darcy nodded at Molly's old riding friends. And even though she was concerned about how bad Molly was feeling, she couldn't help noticing that both of them had been eyeing Tony, as if trying to figure out who he belonged to.

"Let's get out of here," Molly said tightly. "I'm sorry I came."

Wordlessly, Tony started the pickup and pulled out.

Twenty minutes later, when they pulled into Foxfire Stables, Kenny was waiting for them. "Finally get to meet the great horse," he said, grinning at Molly as Darcy and Tony helped her into her chair.

"He's just an ordinary horse," said Molly, her voice still bitter and unhappy. But Darcy saw that when Ebony was led out of the trailer and walked over towards Molly, there were tears of love in her eyes. Tony brought the horse closer to Molly and he lowered his head, sniffing her face and lap.

"You didn't forget me, did you old boy?" she said to him.

"Yep, he knows who his owner is," said Kenny, rubbing Ebony's shoulder.

"I'm not going to ride him," announced Molly, still stroking her horse.

"No, you're not," said Kenny. Molly glanced at him in surprise.

"You heard me," Kenny said. "First of all, you have to get your doctor's permission. Then, an expert has to ride him to determine if he's gentle enough for you. Then, you and he both have a lot to learn. Because most of what you already know you can throw out the window."

"Well, that's all very nice," Molly said, "if I wanted to ride him. But I don't."

Kenny laughed. "We'll see. For now, we'll put Tony on Ebony first, then me," said Kenny.

"That sounds fine," said Molly. "As long as it's not me."

Darcy pushed Molly behind as they followed Tony, Kenny and Ebony into the barn, where Tony bridled and then saddled the horse with a regular English saddle, safety stirrups and fleece pads to cover the seat.

Finally, Tony mounted him. Ebony danced around a bit, but Tony urged the horse forward towards the arena.

"Open the gate Darcy!" Tony yelled.

When Darcy opened it, Tony rode Ebony in small tight circles for a few minutes, talking softly to him. Soon Ebony stopped snorting and prancing and calmly walked around the ring. Then, he started snorting again.

"Poor guy, he hasn't been ridden in so long he's hyper," said Molly watching with round eyes from her wheelchair.

"He's gorgeous, Molly," Darcy said, watching Tony put Ebony through her paces.

"That's because you're not on him," Molly said. "If you were, you'd be scared to death."

"True," Darcy said. "Very true. But I notice you're not."

Molly didn't reply.

After about a half hour, Tony got off and helped Kenny on. Kenny sat beautifully on Ebony, and got him to trot nicely around the arena. Darcy saw that Molly was gaping at them in surprise.

"What's the matter?" Darcy asked, a note of concern in her voice.

"He looks normal on a horse!" said Molly. "Like totally normal!"

"That could be you," Tony said, taking up a place near Molly and Darcy.

"Molly, come in here!" called Kenny.

Darcy pushed Molly's wheelchair through the soft earth into the middle of the arena. Ebony's ears perked up when he saw her.

"Now I want you to watch what I do with my fingers, and how I sit," Kenny shouted, as Ebony cantered around. "You don't have control of your seat anymore, so you're going to use your upper torso to control which way the horse goes."

Darcy watched Molly pay complete attention to what Kenny was saying.

"Then you're going to hold the reins lightly, like this," he demonstrated holding the reins laced between two fingers.

"No," Molly said, *"you're* going to hold the reins lightly."

"Whatever," Kenny said. "When you want to stop him, the pressure is very light, like this. And when you want him to walk out, you let out the reins and shake them lightly." Ebony moved forward at the command, and Kenny grinned at Molly and said, "See? He already knows!"

"I wouldn't go that far, Kenny," said Molly, but she smiled up at him.

"Come on, Molly. He's a quick study and so are you," said Kenny confidently.

Darcy leaned against the fence, watching, wondering how she could convince Molly that she was capable of doing anything Kenny could do on Ebony, maybe even more.

Kenny rode Ebony around a little longer, and then came to a stop next to Molly. "How's that? We'll have him trained for you in no time."

"Don't bother," said Molly. "Train him for yourself, though."

Kenny leaned down and looked at her seriously. Then Darcy heard him speak so softly that she was sure he thought no one could hear.

"Molly," she heard him say, "I know this is tough. It's the toughest thing you've ever gone through in your life. Each time I get on a horse I remember how easy it used to be for me. But this is the way it is now, and there's not a damned thing I can do to change it."

Tears came to Molly's eyes as she looked up at him. But when she spoke, her tone was hard.

"Kenny, train him for yourself if that's want you want. I'm not riding."

"Would you want me to bring you down here by yourself some time," he asked, his eyes soft and searching. "Maybe we could talk about it some more."

Molly's face clouded and she shook her head. "No. No thanks. Hey Darcy, let's get going!" she called.

"Mmmm, great brownies," mumbled Molly, her mouth full. She sat in the family room chair in front of the TV.

"New recipe," Darcy said. "I cut it out of *Muscle and Fitness.*"

"Try it again tomorrow; I think it could use some refinement." Molly grinned. *Well, that's better,* Darcy thought. *At least her attitude is improving. When we left the stables she was in the foulest mood I've ever seen.*

They were watching the six o'clock local news. Molly said she was worn out by their day at Foxfire, but Darcy saw that for the first time in months there was some color in her friend's cheeks. The weather report came on, and Darcy's thoughts drifted back to their afternoon.

I can't push the issue of riding anymore, Darcy thought. *It's up to Molly—and maybe to Kenny. For the moment, the less said the better. She's just going to come to it on her own—that is, if she comes to it at all.*

Darcy's thoughts were interrupted by the newscaster's voice. "This just in. A fire broke out late this afternoon at Foxfire Stables on Sunset Island. Officials are not sure what caused the blaze, but part of the barn area is damaged. 'Fortunately,' said a Foxfire representative, 'the horses were all in the pasture at the time and no horses or people were injured.'"

Molly dropped her brownie in her lap, her face white. "Give me the telephone," she ordered Darcy. Darcy handed her the portable phone.

Molly quickly phoned Foxfire. Kenny answered and assured her that Ebony was fine. No, they still didn't know how the fire had started.

"I can't believe it," Molly said after she hung up. "I moved Ebony because I thought it would be better for him. Now look!"

"It was just an accident, I'm sure, Molly," said Darcy. *Oh yeah?* Darcy heard her own voice in her head. *If you're so sure it's an accident, why do you feel so worried?*

Darcy walked into her criminology class and looked around for Tony. She saw him staring out the window forlornly. *He must be depressed about the fire,* Darcy figured.

She moved up behind him and put her hands over his eyes. "Tony, guess who?"

He turned around and looked sadly into her eyes. "Hi, Darcy. I was just thinking about . . . the fire."

"I guessed that," she said.

"Oh, yeah—I forgot you're telepathic," he said trying to smile.

"I don't need ESP to read your face," she said, moving closer to him.

His expression was strange, one she hadn't seen before. "Are you okay?" she asked, searching his face.

"Oh, sure. You know that nobody was hurt," he said, a small smile crossing his face.

"I know, but you looked so bummed out, I just thought—" Darcy stammered.

"I am bummed out," Tony said. "But barn fires are pretty common because of all that stacked, dry hay. It can spontaneously combust."

"Sounds like you know all about it," Darcy said.

Tony's expression darkened and he stared out the window again. "Yeah, well, I've heard of it before." Then he turned to her and smiled. "Had any fire dreams lately?"

"No, I haven't," she replied. *But I've dreamed about you,* she thought, shuddering a little from the memory.

"Sweet ones, I hope!" Tony said softly. *Not exactly,* Darcy thought to herself, but kept her mouth shut.

The other students took their seats. Darcy and Tony sat near each other towards the front. Professor Aaron was teaching a case history of a teenager who had raped and nearly murdered a girl in New York City, and left her to die. It was a case that Darcy remembered hearing about, but she hadn't known anything about the rapist.

It made her sick to hear that the person who had done it came from a home without a father and with a mother who was an alcoholic, and who didn't seem to care about anybody. *Isn't there any justice in the world?* Darcy thought. *The guy's a criminal, but his life was over by the time he was five years old!*

When the bell sounded ending class, Tony turned to Darcy. "Do you want to go for a Coke? You look like you need it."

"Thanks. Sometimes hearing about all these criminals is really depressing," she said, as they walked out into the gray day to Tony's car—his motorcycle wasn't much good in the rain, he told Darcy.

"You don't like criminals?" Tony joked.

"Let's just say I try to avoid them," Darcy joked back. Tony opened the door for her, and Darcy climbed in.

They drove to The Java coffee shop and found their usual table.

"How's Molly doing?" Tony asked her as they sat down. "Did she get freaked by the fire?"

"A little," Darcy admitted. "She's really attached to that horse, even if she won't ride him."

"Well, that's typical," Tony said, as the waitress took their order. "I've seen it happen many times before."

"Really?" Darcy asked.

"Sure," Tony said, "I've been around horses my whole life. Molly's really scared," Tony continued. "She'll have to figure out that she has to go back and start at the beginning. I'd hate to do that."

"She won't even think about it," said Darcy, as the waitress put her soda in front of her.

"Maybe not for a while," Tony said. "It takes a while." Darcy noticed the waitress, a pretty, dark-haired student, eyeing Tony.

"She'll come back to her old self, I'm sure," said Tony pleasantly. "Doesn't she have any old friends? What about those two we met at Sunset Stables?"

"Jenny and Rowena," Darcy said, taking a sip of soda. "Used to be her best buddies. Not anymore. She basically dropped them."

He nodded, smiled and took her hand. "Sure. It makes perfect sense. Being around them probably reminded her too much of what things used to be like."

"Yeah, that's it," said Darcy. She sipped her drink and glanced at her watch. "Wow, I've gotta go." She rose to leave, and Tony got up, too.

"Can I give you a ride home?" Tony asked. "I wanted to check on the horses over there anyhow."

"Oh, sure," said Darcy. "I didn't drive today."

Tony and Darcy caught the ferry and he dropped her at the Masons', giving her a tender kiss before he drove off. As Darcy walked up the path to the house, she thought about how weird life was. *Exhibit A: Two weeks ago, Tony Mendez wasn't even part of my world. And now, I don't know if I can go for five minutes without thinking about him. Let's face it: I'm crazy about him!*

SIX

"What's up?" asked Molly when she wheeled into Darcy's bedroom that evening.

Darcy sat at her desk, intent on a letter she was typing. "I got the greatest idea," she told Molly. "I'm writing a letter to the *Washington Post.*"

"You're protesting their editorial policies or something?"

"Very funny," Darcy said. "Remember when Tony told us his birthday was coming up this month?"

"Yeah," Molly said. "So?"

"So I am planning a very cool surprise," Darcy said, slipping her typed letter into an envelope. "Remember I told you he used to write for the *Washington Post?* Well, I just wrote to the paper and asked them to send me copies of some of Tony's old articles so I can make a scrapbook for him."

"Don't you think he's already got them somewhere?" asked Molly, absently curling some hair around one finger.

"He doesn't have any because I asked to see them already," said Darcy triumphantly. "He said he was traveling around too much to keep track of them."

"Ah, the nomad's life," Molly said dramatically.

"He's done so much," Darcy mused. "It's really amazing, huh?"

"Amazing," Molly agreed.

"In fact, just about everything about Tony is amazing, don't you think?" Darcy asked eagerly.

"Oh, absolutely," Molly teased. "I think of him as a sort of god, myself."

"Good," Darcy said insouciantly. "I guess that makes me his god-dess!"

Molly pretended to put her finger down her throat and Darcy heaved a pillow at her.

"Watch out!" Molly warned, throwing the pillow back. "Love is making you really stupid!"

Darcy trudged up the hill to the Masons' house after school the next day and saw an expensive rental car parked in the drive. *Wonder who that is,* she thought. *Must be some of the Masons' horror movie friends from New York or something.*

She walked inside and heard laughter echoing through the cavernous front hall.

"Oh, I remember them!" Darcy heard Molly exclaim from the living room, then a deeper, male laughter followed hers.

"Well, hi there!" Darcy said when she walked into the living room. She was surprised to see Howie Lawrence sitting on the couch. He was a nice guy whose family had a summer house on the island.

"Hi," Howie said. "Great to see you again."

"You, too," Darcy said, sitting in a chair near Molly. "What brings you to the island off-season?"

"Oh, Dad asked me to pick something up from the house," Howie said, "and I thought I'd stop by." Howie looked at Molly and blushed a little.

Darcy smiled to herself. Howie had started hanging around Molly over the summer; the two of them had even judged an island Olympics for charity together. But the summer had come to an end, and Howie had left to go back to college at New York University.

"You guys want anything?" Darcy asked, getting up from the chair.

"You don't have to play hostess," Molly said. "I already offered."

Howie was studying a framed picture on the coffee table. It had been taken a year earlier—Molly, seated atop Ebony, grinned confidently into the camera.

"I didn't know you rode," Howie said to Molly with surprise.

"I used to," Molly said, something turning off in her face. "I don't anymore."

"There's a new stable on the island," Darcy put in smoothly. "It's called Foxfire. Molly has her horse there now."

"Are you riding at all?" Howie asked, glancing self-consciously at Molly's legs. His eyes quickly found their way back to her face.

"No," Molly said. "Never again."

"You know, I read somewhere . . . something about paraplegics being able to ride. . . ." Howie mused.

"There's a program at Foxfire, actually," Darcy said.

"Oh yeah?" Howie said. "Sounds cool! You gonna try it?"

"Nope," Molly said. "I've been out there, heard the spiel, and I'll just stay here, thank you very much."

"How come?" Howie asked earnestly.

Molly's face hardened. "Look, I used to be great on a horse, okay? And the idea of riding again in some bogus cripples' program . . ."

"I don't think it's like that," Darcy said mildly.

"Look, I'm gonna be around all weekend," Howie said. "I'd love to go to Foxfire with you and meet your horse."

"Do you ride?" Molly asked with surprise. Howie was a really nice guy, and really rich to boot, but he had a slightly nerdy quality to him and didn't seem like the athletic type.

"Hey, I might be a snotty kid from the suburbs, but I can ride," Howie said. He glanced at his watch and got up. "I gotta run. Can I call you about going over to Foxfire tomorrow?"

"Well, you can call me," Molly allowed.

"Great!" Howie said, grinning at Molly happily. "It'll be a blast!" He kissed Molly on the cheek and waved at Darcy, then bounded for the front door.

"I didn't say we'd go riding," Molly called after him.

"Yes, you did!" he called back.

Molly stared at Darcy. "Did you put him up to that?"

"I didn't! I swear I didn't!" Darcy exclaimed, flopping down on to the couch.

"He's nice, isn't he?" Molly said softly.

"He's really nice!" Darcy agreed. "And he's clearly crazy about you."

Molly raised her eyebrows at Darcy. "Would you please wipe that delighted look off your face?"

"Who me?" Darcy asked innocently. She got up from the couch and stretched. "I'm going to take a hot shower."

"I'll just read over the information my physical therapist sent over about my learning to ride again," Molly said casually.

"You will?" Darcy asked, halfway to the door.

"Yeah," Molly said. "Just in case Howie actually calls me."

"You know he's going to call you," Darcy said. "Besides, as you are always telling me, you can always call him."

"I hate it when you throw my good advice in my face," Molly grumbled.

Darcy blew Molly a kiss and ran out the door, happiness bubbling over inside of her.

Molly was going to ride!

SEVEN

"I don't see any reason why you can't ride, Molly," said Dr. Erikson, Molly's physician. It was Saturday morning, and Darcy and Molly had made a special trip into Portland to see Molly's neurologist.

"You're in good health," he continued, "and I think horseback riding will be good for you."

Darcy grinned at Molly. "I guess there's nothing stopping you now."

"Full speed ahead, huh?" said Molly laughing. But Darcy sensed nervousness in Molly's giggles.

* * *

Not five minutes after they got home from the doctor's office, the phone rang. It was Howie calling to ask if he could take Molly out to the stables.

"Great timing," Molly told him. "I just got my doctor's okay to try the riding program."

Howie drove over to the Masons' and he and Molly left in the specially-equipped van. Darcy made plans to go over to the stables in the afternoon with Tony after getting some homework out of the way.

"Darcy, I've got to hand it to you," Tony said an hour later, "I wouldn't have believed Molly would go without a fight—and without you!"

"Hey, I didn't do a thing," Darcy said. "Give the credit where it's due. To Howie Lawrence. If it weren't for him, Molly would never have done it."

"Give yourself a little credit," Tony said, as he gave Darcy a soft kiss. Darcy felt an electric thrill shoot through her.

"Okay," Darcy said, "if it means that you'll kiss me again." Tony kissed her again, and Darcy had a hard time pulling herself back to reality.

"Tony, I'm going to let you kiss me one more time, and then we are going to get in the truck and go to the stables," Darcy murmured, with a smile on her face.

"You got it," Tony said, his dark brown eyes looking directly into Darcy's.

Actually, I could spend the rest of the day right here, Darcy thought to herself. *I really could. As long as I was with him!*

Darcy spotted Molly and Howie near the Foxfire arena as she and Tony drove up. When they climbed out of the pickup truck, they could see Kenny and Ina giving a riding lesson in the ring to four paraplegic children. Tony and Darcy joined Molly and Howie at the side of the ring. The kids on horseback were guiding the horses at a walk around the ring, each with two helpers flanking their sides. The horses looked docile.

"Now if they can do it you can do it," said Tony, giving Molly a hug in greeting.

"That's what Howie keeps telling me," Molly said, grinning at Howie. "But I keep telling him that I can do it better. What about you, O great Laken? If I do this, you gonna do it too?"

Darcy shook her head vehemently. "No way. I'm scared to death of horses."

Tony looked at her closely. "Oh, come on. You're not scared of anything else."

"Horses are different," she said.

"That's right, they have four legs," Tony said. They all laughed, even Darcy.

Tony slipped an arm affectionately around Darcy's shoulders. "There's no reason you can't be a great rider," he said.

'Yes, there is," Darcy said. "I won't get on a horse."

The kids' riding lesson finished, and Ina led the horses and children to the barn.

Tony turned to Darcy. 'Your turn."

Darcy backed away from him in horror. "No way!"

"Come on. Show Molly how," Tony urged.

"Yeah, Darcy. Set a good example for Molly," urged Howie.

Molly joined in. 'Yeah, Darcy, you can do it."

Darcy, who usually couldn't be coerced into doing anything, found herself being walked by Tony out to where the horses were being held, just inside the barn at the disabled mounting ramp. *I can't believe I'm doing this,* she thought to herself. *Okay, so what if I'm scared to death?*

Darcy saw Kenny standing by one of the horses. "They won't shut up until I do it," she said nervously. "So let's just do it."

Kenny didn't look his usual upbeat self, and kept glancing over towards Molly and Howie.

"It'll be like nothing you've done before," said Kenny, as Ina helped Darcy into the saddle. "Okay, this horse's name is Freckles and he won't hurt you, I guarantee it."

Yeah, like there's anything I can do if he bolts! Darcy found herself about to say. But instead she gritted her teeth and grabbed tightly onto the reins.

Ina led Freckles around the ring, and Darcy held on for dear life. But then something miraculous happened. She started to relax. A little. Then Tony took the lead from Ina, and Darcy relaxed even more. The swaying motion of the horse was gentle, like rocking in a boat. Tony led Darcy and Freckles out to the arena. Darcy managed a sickly grin.

"It's not so bad," said Darcy. "But not up there on my all-time list of most-fab things to do."

"You're just not used to it," Tony said.

"I hope I never get used to it," Darcy replied.

"You're cracking jokes, that's a good sign," Tony shot back, as he led Darcy around the ring. "Try sitting up straight. You might as well take advantage of the view."

Darcy sat higher and glanced to the left. She was amazed to see Molly on one of the other schooling horses. Howie was on one side, and Ina was on the other. Molly was riding!

"This is the weirdest feeling, or lack of feeling," Molly declared as Kenny directed Ina to lead her horse, Amigo, into the arena.

Kenny gazed up at her seriously. 'Yeah, you can forget about using your lower body. Lean left or right to turn him, and light pressure on those reins!"

"Guess I've got no need for spurs, huh?" joked Molly.

"Did you ever?" Kenny replied, an irritated tone in his voice.

What's that all about? Darcy mused, as Tony continued to lead her around. And then it dawned on her. It was

Howie Lawrence. *Kenny doesn't like competition. Can't say I blame him.*

"Kenny, lighten up, will you? I can handle this," Molly said, urging the horse into a trot.

"Don't push it, Molly," Kenny said.

The horse trotted gently around the ring with Molly.

"She looks great, doesn't she?" exclaimed Howie. Molly grinned at him, but Kenny only nodded solemnly.

"Time's up," said Kenny. "Half hour maximum."

"Forever?" asked Molly.

"Just today," said Kenny quietly. "You'll be able to increase time soon."

"Are you helping me off or should I just jump into a helpless heap on the ground?" Molly joked.

Kenny didn't laugh. "Go over to the ramp—it's a whole lot easier."

Molly headed over to the ramp. She looked over at Howie and gave him a quick thumbs-up sign. He grinned back at her broadly.

Howie and Ina led Molly and the horse over to the mounting area, and Ina and Darcy helped her off into her wheelchair. *Ina hasn't said a thing through the whole lesson,* Darcy thought to herself. *What's her problem?*

"You okay?" Howie asked Molly solicitously, after Molly was settled in her chair.

"Sure, no problem," she said, all smiles.

"Okay if I ride for a while before we're outta here?" Howie asked. "Or do you want to go?"

"Hey, I said no problem," Molly repeated, still grinning broadly. Howie walked over to the horses and saddled one up.

"Someday you'll probably be able to ride with him," said Darcy.

"Not for a while, though," added Kenny, who had made his way over towards Molly and was eyeing her protectively.

Uh-oh, Darcy thought. *What we've got going here is a love triangle in the making. Well, it'll make life interesting for Molly. I wonder if she even notices that she's the one in the middle.*

* * *

Back at the Masons' house, Darcy and Tony strolled up the front path a couple of minutes after unloading Molly. Howie had said he'd get Molly up to the house. He was true to his word: When Darcy and Tony approached, they saw him holding Molly in his arms at the front door. He was kissing her.

"Is he carrying her over the threshold?" quipped Darcy.

"I don't know, but it looks pretty romantic to me," said Tony, giving her hand a squeeze.

"Molly's probably in heaven," said Darcy.

Howie put Molly back in her chair and turned to face Tony and Darcy. "Great day, huh?" he said, a grin on his face. "I'll see you guys later."

"Later," said Tony.

They watched as Howie made his way to his car and drove off. Molly said, "Wow, who would think I could ride a horse like that?"

"Amigo or Howie?" Darcy quipped.

"Shaddup," said Molly. But she was smiling.

"You and I should go riding sometime, Molly," said Tony.

"Hey, I'd love it. Let's go!" said Molly enthusiastically. "Darcy, too."

"As long as you guys give me a crash helmet," said Darcy.

Darcy wheeled Molly into the house and brought her upstairs. Then she and Tony went to sit on the swing in the Masons' yard. They were quiet for a time.

"*Qué hay?*" Tony finally said.

"Huh?" said Darcy.

"It's Spanish for 'what's up,'" Tony explained, putting his arm around Darcy. "You were a million miles away."

Darcy snuggled against him. "Just thinking about how hilarious it is that both Howie and Kenny are after Molly."

His deep brown eyes searched hers. "Do you ever not think about Molly?"

"Probably never," said Darcy, chuckling. "She's a big part of my life."

"What about me?" Tony asked, holding Darcy even closer. He turned her lips to his and kissed her. Darcy closed her eyes and let herself float—the feel of Tony's arms around her waist, her fingers entwined in his rich dark hair, were all she wanted. *Maybe all I ever want,* she considered, and then gave herself back over to a tumble of delicious feelings.

"Those jodhpurs in there—the gray ones—yes, perfect!" cried Molly excitedly.

It was a couple days later, and Molly had undergone a remarkable transformation—the girl who wouldn't even think about riding her horse now seemed ready to get into shape for the Kentucky Derby.

Darcy had pulled what seemed like dozens of pairs of riding pants out of Molly's closet. Molly had them laid out on her bed and was examining each pair. "The gray ones are it," she declared. "With the red checked shirt."

"Are you absolutely sure about this, Miss Krone?" joked Darcy, tossing out the name of a famous female jockey. She flung a handful of clothes up in the air.

Molly giggled. "Yes, totally. Now come and help me into them."

Darcy had had plenty of practice at dressing Molly, but she had never dealt with jodhpurs before. The seams got twisted easily and the patches kept appearing on the wrong parts of Molly's legs.

Molly sighed dramatically. "Darcy, the patches go on the inside of the knee."

"I'm trying," Darcy said. "I'm trying."

"So try harder," Molly grinned. "Tony's picking us up in ten minutes." Darcy finally got Molly into her jodhpurs just as the doorbell rang.

"What did I tell you?" asked Molly. "I knew it."

"Golly Miss Molly, I'll go see who it is," Darcy said, leaving Molly to finish dressing herself.

Since it was Simon's day off, she skipped downstairs and opened the front door. But it wasn't Tony. Instead, Darcy found herself looking at a guy in a wheelchair.

"Kenny, what a surprise!" she said, and let him wheel himself into the Masons' house. *Uh-oh,* Darcy thought. *Get ready for Standard Reaction to the Mason House #1.* Darcy looked at Kenny. *Yep.* His mouth hung open in amazement.

"What is this place? Some kind of morgue?" he asked, staring at the skull wallpaper and an arrangement of skulls in the foyer.

"Nah, it's post-modern decorating," Darcy quipped. "Molly's parents write horror movies."

"Gee, what a shocker," Kenny joked. "So they like to be in an environment conducive to their work, is that it?"

This time Darcy laughed. "Something like that," she said, "something like that. Where's Tony? I thought he was coming over."

"Tony was giving a lesson, so I came. I have a van like Molly's," he said, smiling. He picked up a stray skull and considered it quizzically.

"I'm glad you came," said Darcy warmly. "Molly's almost ready. We'll be down in a minute."

"Tell her to boogie," he said, cupping his hands around his mouth so that his voice echoed up the staircase. Then he laughed like Dracula, and the laughter echoed through the house like in a horror movie.

Darcy went upstairs to get Molly, and finally they were ready to go.

"What do you guys think about going to the Play Café later?" Kenny asked as he pulled out of the driveway.

"Sure," said Molly and Darcy at the same time.

"Okay, it's a triple date," Kenny said. "Me and two gorgeous ladies. Must be my lucky day."

"What the hell's going on here?" Kenny mumbled under his breath, as he turned the van into the Foxfire driveway. There was a strange-looking truck in the parking lot, and a lot of people running around.

"Who is that?" asked Molly straining forward in her seat.

"It's the vet's truck," said Kenny. "Wonder what he's doing here."

Darcy hopped out of the van and helped Molly out. Kenny used the van's special equipment to lower his wheelchair. When Molly was out, Darcy ran over to the vet's truck. Kenny and Molly wheeled themselves over quickly.

"What's the problem, Doc Thompson?" asked Kenny.

Dr. Thompson didn't look up from the box of medicines he was rummaging through.

"What's going on?" repeated Darcy.

Dr. Thompson kept looking for medicines as he spoke. "Four horses sick, probably poisoned. Now please stay out of my way," he said, deadly serious.

"No kidding!" exclaimed Kenny.

"Why would anyone do that?" asked Darcy in horror.

"Nothing in the paddocks and barn they could have eaten," said the vet. "Had to be some sicko did it."

"Which horses?" asked Molly, a look of horror crossing her face.

"Two of the grays, Freckles and that big bay, Big Boy," said the doctor.

"Oh, that's awful!" cried Darcy.

Kenny's face fell. The vet found what he was looking for and started walking quickly back to the barn. They all followed him.

"How do you think they were poisoned?" Kenny asked.

"Probably rat poison in their grain or something. The police were already called. Awful way to die," Dr. Thompson said gravely.

They made their way to the barn where they had to stop. Dr. Thompson went to work on a horse lying just inside the barn. Tony was holding the horse's head comfortingly in his arms. He didn't even notice his friends watching from outside.

"Oh God, it's Randy," gasped Kenny. Tears coursed down his cheeks.

"Isn't that the one you were riding the other day, Kenny?" asked Molly.

Kenny could only nod. Molly burst into tears, and took his hand in hers.

Darcy gazed helplessly at Tony, who stroked the horse's neck. "Poor Randy, poor old horse. We're going to try to make you feel better now."

Dr. Thompson pressed his hand against the horse's neck to take his pulse, then quickly held the bell of his stethoscope against the horse's chest. Darcy watched him in alarm.

Then the stall fell strangely quiet. Tony stopped cooing to the horse. The horse's harsh breathing eased.

"This one's dead," said the vet to Tony. "I've done all I can. Nothing to do now but wait for the police." The two of them walked slowly out of the barn.

Darcy, Kenny and Molly fell in step with them as they made their way back to the vet's van. They were trying to hold back tears, Doc Thompson included. They heard a siren wail in the distance, and Darcy knew that the police were arriving. *Too late,* she thought bitterly, *too late. Who would do such a sick thing?*

Darcy looked at Tony. He was frowning through his tears. "Look, there's Ina," he said.

Darcy followed his gaze. Ina was standing like a frightened animal near the main gate. Then, Ina darted towards the woods.

What is she running away from? Darcy asked herself. *Does she have something to do with all of this?*

EIGHT

Before she could stop and think about what she was doing, Darcy ran into the woods after Ina. She darted through the thick foliage, blocking branches from her face with her shoulders and hands. *What was that?* She glimpsed something white up ahead—*Ina's shirt?* Darcy ran towards what turned out to be a plastic shopping bag speared to a branch. Breathing hard, she listened for a moment. *Yes! The sound of twigs cracking!* Stealthily, she moved towards the sound.

There was Ina! But she flitted behind a tree and quickly went deeper into the woods. *God, she's fast,* thought Darcy. *If only I knew these woods as well as she does. . . .*

Darcy bounded ahead, gaining on the girl, yet Ina didn't let up. In a semi-clearing, Darcy sprinted, lunging for Ina. She caught the girl by one thin arm and dragged her to the ground.

"Don't hurt me!" Ina yelped in fear.

"I'm not going to hurt you," Darcy said. She helped Ina to her feet but held on to her firmly. "I just want to know why you're running away."

Ina's face, half covered with her long, tangled blond hair, was white with fear. "I d-didn't d-do anything," she stammered.

"So why were you running?"

"I . . . don't know," Ina mumbled, staring miserably at the ground.

Darcy sighed. "Look, I'm not trying to hurt you or scare you, okay? Just tell me what happened to the horses."

"I don't know anything about it; I didn't see anything." Ina wagged her head furiously, still struggling against Darcy's tight grasp.

"Hey, Ina, you didn't run away for no reason at all," Darcy said. She held firmly to Ina's arm. "It'll be a lot easier if you just tell the truth."

"I don't like the cops, okay?" Ina spit out, shaking her lank hair out of her eyes.

"Well, that's too bad, because I have a feeling they're going to arrive any minute," Darcy said. She began to lead the girl back towards the clearing. She felt her resist, and saw that she was ready to make a break for it. "Don't try it," Darcy warned. "All it'll get you is tackled again."

"Hi," Tony called as soon as they hit the clearing. He ran over to them and gave Darcy a hug. "What happened to you?"

"I chased her," Darcy said matter-of-factly.

Tony's eyes flitted from Darcy's face to Ina's and back to Darcy's. "Good work," he said quietly.

"I didn't do anything, Tony!" Ina said vehemently.

"It'll be okay, Ina," Tony said, gentleness coloring his voice. "Come on." He took Darcy's hand, Darcy kept a hold of Ina with her other hand, and the three of them walked across the clearing.

As they came around the other side of the barn, Darcy stopped in her tracks. Across the stable yard, staring at her, was Scott. As Scott focused on their clasped hands, Darcy was suddenly conscious of how close together she and Tony were.

"Hi," Darcy said awkwardly, quickly dropping Tony's hand.

"What are you doing here?" Scott asked.

"I came with Molly—she's in the house," Darcy said.

"You hate horses," Scott said bluntly. "You're scared of them."

"Well—" Darcy began.

"Excuse me, why do I get the feeling you two know each other?" Tony asked.

"We're friends," Darcy mumbled.

"We used to be friends," Scott amended.

"Look, Scott, I—"

"I'm here to investigate a report," Scott said tersely. "So whatever you have to say will have to wait."

I deserved that, Darcy said to herself, staring at the ground. I can't believe I got myself into this mess.

"What happened here?" Scott asked Tony. He had his little black notebook open to a fresh page and was poised to write down anything Tony said.

"I don't know," Tony said, casually reaching for Darcy's hand again. Darcy pulled away slightly, but Tony didn't seem to notice—he just put his arm around Darcy's waist. "Dr. Thompson—the vet—thinks that the horses were poisoned, maybe something put into their feed."

Scott turned his attention to Ina. "What about you?"

"I don't know anything," she said sullenly. "The horses should smell poison in their food, or sense it. They sense everything else," she said.

"Did you feed them?" Scott asked.

"This morning," Ina said. "But that doesn't mean I know anything about this."

"Okay," Scott said, making a note in his book. "You can go."

"You're just going to let her go?" Darcy asked Scott. "I just chased her down because she was running away!"

"Yeah, well, no one asked you to," Scott said coolly. "I'm sure we can find you again if we need you," he added, nodding at Ina.

"She doesn't go too far from the horses," said Tony, giving Ina a compassionate smile.

Ina scurried away, shooting one look backwards before she ran into the barn.

Scott gave Tony an appraising look. "So, what's your story, Mendez? Tell me all about your day," said Scott, tapping his pen against his notebook.

"Just ordinary," said Tony. "I gave a riding lesson this morning. Kenny went to pick up Molly and Darcy, and by the time they got here, the vet was already working on the horses."

"Well, what were *you* doing when Kenny was gone?" Scott demanded.

Tony shrugged. "Like I said—giving a lesson. That's my job."

"Have you seen anything strange around here today?" Scott continued.

"No, not a thing," answered Tony.

"I'd call Ina running away pretty strange," Darcy supplied.

"That's nothing," said Tony. "Ina's just terrified of people."

Scott's eyes were trained on Tony. Scott seemed tense and alert. "So how do you think this happened?"

"Beats me. I think we should check other farms and see if it happened anywhere else. Maybe the water supply is messed up," suggested Tony.

"What makes you think that?" quizzed Scott.

"Nothing special. I just think we should check out every possibility," said Tony. "I mean, no way would someone purposely hurt these horses."

"How do you know?" Scott challenged him. "There are lots of sickos in this world. People have been known to leave poisoned meat out for the neighborhood dogs they don't like."

"Not around here," Tony insisted.

"No offense, buddy, but I don't even know that *you* wouldn't do something like that," Scott said, staring Tony in the eye.

Darcy couldn't take it anymore. "Scott, lay off," she said quietly.

"Excuse me, Miss Laken," Scott said, "You are interfering with official police procedures."

"Look, Scott, I know you're doing your job," said Darcy softly. "But take it easy. He didn't do it."

Tony stared hard at Scott. "Have you got a problem?"

"I'd say it's you who has the problem," Scott shot back.

"What is it you want?" Tony asked Scott. "You want me to say I did it?"

"Did you?" Scott asked.

"Stop it! This is ridiculous!" Darcy yelled. "This is about me acting like a fool and it should be about the crime!"

"Don't flatter yourself," Scott told Darcy in a cold voice, his eyes still trained on Tony. "Are you willing to take a lie detector test?"

Tony sighed deeply and put his arm around Darcy's neck. "Sure, if it'll get you off my back."

"I don't think this is necessary, Scott," said Darcy, with barely concealed fury.

Scott ignored her. A muscle twitched in his cheek as he wrote something down and handed it to Tony. "You can take the lie detector test in Portland tomorrow between nine-thirty and four. Here's the address. I'll let them know you're coming."

Tony slipped the note wordlessly into his pants pocket.

"You're not going to interrogate anyone else?" asked Darcy in amazement.

"I'm going up to the house now, to talk to Kenny. If I need to, I'll call again." Scott gave Darcy one long, hard look, spun on his heel, and strode to his car.

Darcy watched him go.

"What's up with the two of you?" Tony asked.

"God, I'm so sorry," Darcy said, pushing her hair out of her face. "I should have told him about you, and I should have told you about him—"

Tony's face darkened. "I thought he was an old boyfriend, not a current one."

"I've been seeing him for a couple of months," Darcy admitted.

"He's in love with you," Tony said tersely.

"He can't be!" Darcy blurted out. "He's never even kissed me!"

"Like this?" Tony asked in a low voice, then he brought Darcy's face to his and kissed her passionately.

"Like that," Darcy agreed breathlessly.

"I'm glad," Tony said softly. "I don't want anyone else to kiss you like that."

"I'm really sorry about the lie detector test and everything," Darcy said. "Scott's ticked off at me and he's taking it out on you."

"Darcy, I'd do anything for you. Don't you know that by now?"

Tony put his arm around her and kissed her again. It was an unbelievably wonderful feeling. But even as Darcy closed her eyes and gave herself up to the kiss, she saw the horses suffering and the one dying.

And in her heart, she knew there was some terrible evil at Foxfire, just waiting to strike again.

NINE

Darcy strode up to Scott's front door and knocked insistently.

"Who is it?"

"It's me," Darcy said evenly.

Scott peered through the slot afforded by the chain lock, then unhooked it. "What's up?"

"I have to talk to you," she said as she marched into the room and sat down on his familiar threadbare couch.

"So, talk," Scott said, folding his arms in front of him.

"I owe you an apology," Darcy said. "I should have told you about Tony."

"No kidding," Scott said flatly.

"I . . . I don't have a good excuse," Darcy admitted. "I just wussed out."

Scott stared at her, then shook his head ruefully. "It really sucks, Darcy. I thought you were the kind of girl who is always straight with people—"

"I am!"

"Bull," Scott interjected. "Not when the going gets tough."

Darcy stared at the gold pattern in the rug. *He's right,* she thought to herself morosely. *I can't even defend myself, because he's right.*

"So, where'd you meet this guy?" Scott asked.

"At school," she said. "He's not from around here."

"I can tell. I've lived here all my life, remember?" he said with bitterness. "There's something strange about him, Darcy."

"Oh, come on, Scott," Darcy chided, "That's ridiculous!"

"Look, I'm not just saying this because I'm jealous, if that's what you're thinking," Scott insisted.

"Now who isn't being straight?" Darcy asked pointedly.

"Just be careful," Scott warned her.

"Of what?" Darcy exploded. She took a deep breath and vowed to control her temper. "Scott," she continued in a softer voice, "this is silly. Tony is a great guy. I know you don't want to believe that, but it's true."

"Sure," Scott said with disgust.

"I know him, you don't!" Darcy exclaimed. "I saw Tony kneeling by the side of that dying horse. I saw the love on his face, and the tears running down his cheeks. If you had seen what I saw, there's no way you could think he was guilty."

"I don't make decisions based on people's emotional responses, Darcy," Scott said. He took a Coke out of the refrigerator and handed it to Darcy. "It's insubstantial evidence."

She leapt to her feet, spilling some of the Coke from the bottle. "You drive me crazy! How can you say that?"

He shrugged. "Experience."

"Experience?" Darcy exploded. "Gimme a break! You've only been a cop for a year!"

"You are reacting emotionally, per usual," Scott said coolly. "Crimes don't get solved that way."

"Forget it! Just forget the whole thing!" Darcy yelled, storming out of the apartment.

What nerve! Darcy thought as she started the car. *He is so infuriating!*

Instead of going straight home, Darcy turned towards the Sunset Country Club, where the Mason family had a membership. Molly would hardly ever go anymore, but Darcy still went alone occasionally to swim and to practice her dives from the highboard. She had thrown her swimsuit in the car earlier and thought it would probably feel good to cool off a bit. The pool was practically empty. Most of the members of the club were summer residents, which meant that the pool was never crowded off-season.

She dove in cleanly, and swam until she felt her muscles relaxing.

Then she realized a male voice was calling to her. She stopped swimming and looked up to see the handsome face of Kurt Ackerman, head swimming instructor. Kurt was a sophomore in college and he'd grown up on the island. Darcy had gotten to be good friends with Kurt's girlfriend, Emma Cresswell, a Boston heiress who worked on the island as an au pair during the summers.

"Hey, how's life in the fast lane?" Darcy asked, swimming over to Kurt.

"School, two jobs, and Emma away at college," Kurt said, sitting by the edge of the pool. "In other words, it sucks."

"You miss her, huh?" Darcy asked.

"Yeah," Kurt said with a sigh. "I got a letter from her today, though. I think she's coming to visit soon!"

"Oh, great!" Darcy said. "Hey, tell her to call me and Molly when she gets here, okay?"

"If I can bear to share her, I will," Kurt said with a grin, "but don't count on it." He waved good-bye and headed for his office.

Kurt feels about Emma the way I feel about Tony, Darcy sighed to herself, floating on her back dreamily. *And the way Scott feels about you,* a voice added in her head. How did life get so complicated?

That night, Darcy fell asleep almost instantly. She dreamed about the horse dying. Tony was kneeling beside it stroking its mane. Darcy knelt down beside him, and he gave her a look of such abject sadness, that she wanted to reach out and hold him, to somehow make everything okay.

She opened her mouth to offer words of comfort, but no sound came out of her mouth. And then Tony's mouth opened, wider and wider, until Darcy was looking into a dark, bloody cavern. Now she couldn't move, couldn't speak, and the cavern grew bigger and bigger until there was no horse and no Tony. And then from far away a faint frightened voice called to her: "Stop me—please stop me!"

And as Darcy opened her mouth, struggling to get out the words "Stop who? Who are you?" a bodiless face flew at her, its mouth open in a stark, silent scream.

It was Ina.

Darcy awoke with a start bathed in sweat, breathing hard. "But what does it mean?" she asked out loud in frustration. "I have to know!"

But there was no answer, only the sound of her heart hammering in the darkness.

TEN

"Does this make you nervous?" Darcy asked Tony the next day as they drove along Congress Street in Portland towards the offices of International Law Enforcement Assistance, Inc.

He smiled easily. "It'd make me nervous if I'd done anything, but since I didn't, I'm not worried."

"Well I'm glad you're handling it so well," Darcy said, as she watched for the address of ILEA. "If someone made me take one of those things, I'd be nervous regardless!"

"Dr. Aaron talked a little about lie detectors in class, remember?" Tony said. "He said they're not admissible as criminal evidence, anyway."

"I thought you said you're not a criminal," Darcy replied, teasing him.

"Only interested in stealing your heart," Tony shot back, a twinkle in his eye.

"Corny, but it's stolen," Darcy admitted. "So who do you think could have done it?"

Tony bit his lower lip. "Don't know. Maybe Ina, but I guess there's no real proof."

"I think it's her," Darcy said. "Besides the fact that she ran away, I've just got a feeling."

"Maybe it's some outsider," Tony said. "I mean, that poison could have been left in the barn for a long time before the horses ate it."

"Maybe," said Darcy, noncommittally. As she spoke, she had a quick flash of her last dream about Tony. *What could that possibly have been about? It just doesn't make any sense.*

"I really hope those other three horses are okay," Tony said suddenly, pulling Darcy out of her reverie.

"The vet said they were okay, didn't he?" asked Darcy.

"Well, he said they'll live, but he didn't know how well they'd recover. They might be useless for the paraplegic program."

As they rounded a turn and the ILEA building came into view, Darcy asked, "Aren't you even the slightest bit nervous, Tony?"

"No, should I be?" he asked, smiling at her. "It's not a big deal, Darcy." He slid an arm around her shoulders.

"It's just that they'll treat you like a criminal for coming in here," she said.

"No, they won't," said Tony, parking the car. "Innocent until proven guilty, remember? Besides, these aren't cops. This is a private company. They do these every day."

A well-dressed young woman was sitting behind a reception desk in an expensively decorated outer office when Tony and Darcy entered the ILEA building. She greeted them with a smile. "What can I do for you?" she asked.

"I'm here to take a lie detector test," announced Tony, handing her the paper Scott had given him.

The woman took the paper and read it. The phone rang. "Okay, we'll take you in a minute," she said brightly, reaching for the receiver. "Have a seat."

Darcy felt all tight inside, but Tony was grinning as if he were six years old and watching cartoons on television.

"Look, don't worry so much. What the polygraph lie detector does is record physical reactions to questions," explained Tony. "If you have a certain kind of reaction then you're lying."

"Sounds kind of iffy to me," said Darcy. "It does to me, too, but they still use it," said Tony.

A middle-aged woman dressed in a smart business suit came out to the reception area holding a file. "Mr. Mendez?" she called.

"Right here," Tony said, getting to his feet.

"Follow me, please," the woman said.

"Can my girlfriend come with me?"

He called me his girlfriend, Darcy thought. *Me. His girlfriend.*

"Sure," the woman said. "She can watch from the other side of the window. She might find it educational."

Darcy was led to a seat in a hallway. She looked inside the room. Tony was already sitting down and the woman was attaching several wires to him that came from a machine on a table. It looked a lot like a machine Darcy had seen at the hospital, with a long strip of graph paper running out of one side. She figured that the needle would draw lines on the moving graph paper.

She could hear the questions faintly through the glass. Some of them seemed to be about the incident at the barn, and others seemed totally arbitrary.

"Who won the World Series last year?" the woman asked. Darcy couldn't hear Tony's answer.

"What time did you get to Foxfire that day?" the woman asked.

"About 10:15," Darcy made out. The questioning went on for a while, and when it was over, Tony emerged, confidently.

"Well, how did you do?" Darcy asked.

"The polygraph examiner has to look it over," said Tony. "They'll have the results in about half an hour."

The two of them made their way to a small lounge they had seen near the main reception area. Tony poured coffee for them both.

"So what was it like?" asked Darcy.

"Piece of cake," Tony said. "See, the theory is that if you lie, your breathing, perspiration, and blood pressure change. If you tell the truth, they don't."

"How do you know all this?" Darcy asked, genuinely curious.

"I was indicted for murder a year ago—not!" Tony joked. "Actually I read ahead in our crim book."

"Mr. Mendez?"

The same woman who had administered the polygraph stepped into the lounge. Darcy looked at her closely.

"Mr. Mendez, here's your polygraph result. You passed. We're going to send a copy on to the Sunset Island Police Department. Of course," the woman said, "this is just a preliminary result. But we haven't been wrong yet."

"Great!" Darcy exclaimed, looking at Tony. He was also beaming.

Darcy slapped his palm with her own, then gave him a big hug.

"See? What did I tell you—nothing to worry about."

This'll show Scott, Darcy thought. *He may not like Tony, but he'll have to agree that he's no criminal.*

After Tony dropped her off, Darcy drove over to the Sunset Island police station.

"May I speak to Officer Phillips, please?" she asked the receptionist.

"Let me page him," she said, pressing some buttons.

"I'm right here."

Darcy turned around to face Scott. His blond hair was pressed down under his cap and he looked very serious.

"Oh, hi."

"What can I do for you?" he asked.

Darcy looked around the station. No privacy. "Is there somewhere we can go to talk?"

"Follow me," he said. He led her into a small glass-walled conference. Although they could be observed by anybody who chose to look in, it was quiet. Scott sat down in a big leather chair.

"What's up, Darcy?" he asked, his blue eyes fixed on hers.

"I went with Tony to get the lie detector test today," she began, pacing the room. "And I wanted to tell you personally that he passed with flying colors."

"They called me from Portland," Scott said. "One less suspect on my list. I'm happy, actually."

"Happy?" Darcy asked.

"Sure, I'm glad the guy didn't do it. Aren't you?"

"I never thought he did," Darcy reminded him.

"So he's basically cleared, Scott said, ignoring her. Polygraphs aren't conclusive," Scott said, "but they're pretty darned good."

"What do you mean, not conclusive?" Darcy contended, as she noted two cops bringing a drunk into the station. "You sent him all the way over there to take the stupid test and now you're saying it's not conclusive?"

"Hey, relax!" Scott said, holding his hand up for her to stop. "I'm sorry he had to go to the trouble. It's for his benefit as much as anyone else's. But you can't take those test results as gospel."

"He passed!" Darcy shot back. "Now you're telling me not to believe the test?"

"Hey, Darcy, lighten up," Scott said. "I'm just doing the best job I can on this case. I mean, what do you really know about his guy?"

Darcy stood up. "I don't know. What do you know about me, Scott? Do you have a full report on me, from the FBI maybe?" she challenged.

"I don't need one on you, Darcy," Scott said. "You're not a suspect."

Darcy looked at him for a moment before she spoke. *I better take the bull by the horns here, even if I don't want to.*

"Look, Scott," she said finally, "I think the problem isn't Tony, but that I'm dating Tony. So I think the best we can do right now is stay just friends."

"No," Scott said, "that's not the answer. I don't want to be just friends with you, Darcy. And if I can't have what I want, I don't want to see you."

"That's fine, Scott," Darcy said over her shoulder as she was leaving. "Anyway, if you're interested, I think I know who did it. Give me a call if you want."

ELEVEN

Darcy got into the van and headed for the stables. A plan was formulating in her mind. "Scott, you make me crazy!" she yelled out loud, as if he were with her in the car. When she glanced to the right she saw that the guy in the next car was looking at her curiously. "You're really losing it, Laken," she mumbled, pulling her car ahead of his.

Okay, I've got to handle this myself, Darcy decided, *and that means having a little chat with Ina.* She had a really strong feeling that Ina was guilty. *Didn't she run away? And wasn't she in that horrid nightmare?* Well, she'd have to prove it to Scott; that's all there was to it.

She parked the van in the drive beside the barn. The stables seemed quiet; two horses were in the nearest paddock munching on some hay.

Darcy found Ina brushing a big gray horse, talking to him quietly.

"Hi, Ina," Darcy said, coming up behind her.

Ina jumped and gave Darcy a frightened look. "You scared me."

"How's the horse?" she asked. "Is this one of the ones that was poisoned?"

"I didn't do it," Ina mumbled, staring at the ground.

"I never said that you did it; I just asked about this horse," Darcy said quietly.

89

Ina clutched the grooming brush and kept staring at the ground. She seemed rooted to the spot. "This horse is fine now. He's a nice horse. Nicer than most people."

"Don't you like people?" Darcy asked her gently.

Ina shrugged. "Most people don't like me," she confessed in a low voice.

At that moment, Darcy realized how young Ina looked, her thin, pale face peeking out from behind her stringy hair. "How old are you?"

"Eighteen," Ina replied.

"Do you live with your parents?" asked Darcy.

"They're dead," Ina said flatly.

"I'm sorry," Darcy said sincerely. "It must be hard to be alone."

"Oh, it doesn't matter. I was alone when they were alive, too." She looked at Darcy out of the corner of her eye. "They thought I was nuts and stuck me in a home. You think I'm nuts too, don't you?"

"I don't know what to think," Darcy said honestly. "I think maybe you need help."

"I don't," Ina said, moving even closer to the horse. 'You have to stop accusing me!"

"I'm not accusing you," Darcy said, working to keep her voice even and non-threatening. "Why would I? You haven't done anything wrong, right?"

Ina's eyes grew so large they looked like they might pop out of her head. "No, never!" She laced her fingers through the horse's mane and clung to it, pressing herself against the horse's body.

"Ina, I'm not going to hurt you. Relax," Darcy said. "I'm sorry for what's happened to you, really. And I'm sorry for what's happened to the horses."

"Don't you think I am?" Ina screeched, really looking at Darcy for the first time.

"Yeah, I do," Darcy said softly. "I really do."

Darcy said good-bye and wandered back into the stable. She noticed a room with lots of bottles and jars, probably medicines. *Maybe Ina made a mistake and gave the horses something from one of those jars,* Darcy mused. *Maybe she did it, and it was totally an accident, and now she's too scared to own up to it. God, that poor girl!*

Darcy ran to the front door when she saw Tony from the window. It was evening, and Darcy couldn't wait to see him again.

"Hi," she said, putting her arms around his neck.

"Nice greeting," he said, kissing her softly. "I missed you."

"Ditto," Darcy said, nuzzling into Tony's neck.

"I thought maybe we'd go see a movie, but now I'm having too much fun," he said with a laugh.

"A movie's a great idea," Darcy said. "I've been wanting to see *Hot House Princess,* if you haven't seen it yet."

"Sounds fine," Tony agreed.

Darcy looked outside. "No motorcycle?"

"I decided to give you a break," Tony said, cocking his head towards his Toyota Celica parked in the driveway.

On the way to the movies, Darcy told Tony about her talk with Ina. "Do you think she could've given the horses poison by mistake, maybe instead of a medication?"

Tony shook his head. "Naw. There are no poisons around the barn, and she knows exactly what she's doing with horses. No question."

"But what if poison was put in the wrong container or something?" Darcy pressed.

"That's kind of a long shot, Darcy," said Tony.

"But she's disturbed, I mean really disturbed," Darcy insisted.

"Did you have one of your psychic dreams about her or something?" Tony asked sharply.

"Sort of," Darcy admitted. *You were in it, too,* she added in her mind.

Tony looked at her quickly. "What did you dream?"

Darcy shook her head. "It didn't make any sense."

Tony smiled at her. "Relax, then. I'm sure Scott, the last of the Dudley Do-rights, will catch whoever did it."

"Don't call him that," Darcy said.

"Hey, come on—Scott is Mr. Boring, Darcy. A girl like you would never have been satisfied with him."

"You don't even know him," Darcy mumbled. She stared out the window. *Why am I fighting with Tony, of all people?* she asked herself.

Tony reached over and touched her leg gently, as if he could read her thoughts. "Hey, sorry," he said easily. "All I meant was that Scott is average, and you aren't. And as far as Ina goes, trust me, she wouldn't hurt a flea."

Darcy put her hand over his. Maybe Tony was right. He knew Ina a lot better than she did.

"So, what did you think?" Darcy asked as she and Tony walked out of the movie theater.

"I liked it," Tony said. "Goldie Hawn was great." He wrapped his arm around Darcy's shoulders. "You hungry?"

"Starved," Darcy admitted, kissing his cheek. She felt light-hearted for the first time in days.

They drove to the waterfront and bought fish and chips from a stand, then strolled down the boardwalk happily eating their food.

"What a great night," Darcy said, popping another french fry into her mouth. "It's like Indian summer!"

When they finished eating, she threw their trash away, and pulled Tony towards the water. "Come on!" she urged. "I want to walk on the beach."

"It'll be freezing down there," Tony protested.

"Oh, come on," Darcy chided, pulling on his hand, "I'll keep you warm."

"Wooooh!" Darcy shrieked as she ran along the sand, the wind whipping her hair in her face. "This is fabulous!"

Tony ran next to her, then sprinted ahead, turned around and ran backwards. "Come on, slowpoke!" he called to her over the sounds of the surf.

She ran to him and then he stopped and wrapped his arms around her. Darcy buried her face in his neck, her lips brushing against his hot skin.

"Darcy," he whispered; then he kissed her.

I love this feeling, Darcy thought, eagerly returning his kiss. *I never want it to end. I want us to be like this forever, never stop loving each other. Loving each other* —the thought brought goose pimples to her skin. *Is that what we're doing? Is that what I'm doing?*

"Darcy," Tony said again. His voice sounded rough as he pulled away from her. He stared into her eyes. "I'm falling in love with you. Do you know that?"

"I . . . I don't know what to think," Darcy said in a hushed voice.

"But you feel it too, don't you," Tony insisted.

"I know I've never felt like this before," Darcy told him. "But it's too soon—"

"No, no it isn't," Tony insisted, pressing his fingers into Darcy's arms. He stared at her intensely. "It's wonderful and special. Don't you know that?"

"I do know it's special," Darcy said softly.

Tony smiled and pulled her close again, this time rocking her gently. "I want to travel to Europe with you and show you all the stuff I've seen. You deserve to have great adventures, Darcy."

"It just never seemed possible before," she told him.

"That's one of the terrible things about being poor," Tony acknowledged. "Sometimes it means your dreams stay just that—dreams. But I can make your dreams come true."

"I kind of always thought I could make my own dreams come true," Darcy teased him.

Tony laughed. "You're such a tough girl. How about a compromise—we make our dreams come true together?" And then he bent his head and sealed the deal with a kiss.

It was after midnight when Darcy and Tony drove quietly up to the Masons'. They tiptoed up the walk, so as not to wake anyone. At the front door, Tony pulled Darcy into his arms again. She closed her eyes and pressed her mouth against his, feeling a delicious shiver as his arms tightened around her.

Suddenly the front door opened and banged loudly against the door jamb. Molly sat there and blushed a little as both Darcy and Tony blinked in the sudden bright light.

"Sorry to interrupt, but something terrible has happened," Molly gulped out.

"What is it?" Darcy asked in alarm. "Are you okay?"

"Yeah," Molly said. "But I got a call from Kenny. Someone dug a deadfall trap in the woods and a boy out riding fell into it!"

"Oh my God, is he all right?" asked Darcy. The image of a skull flashed through her head.

"He's okay. He fell on his head, but he had on a riding helmet so he didn't crack his skull open."

Molly's words sent a chill through Darcy.

"He broke his arm, which'll mend," Molly continued bitterly, "but his horse broke a leg and had to be put to sleep."

"That's awful," said Tony, shaking his head. "How sad."

"It's terrible," said Molly. "They're closing the stables until they can figure out what's going on!" Tears shone in her round eyes and Darcy moved over to comfort her. "I just moved Ebony there, and now look what's happening! I'm scared!"

"I'll call Scott first thing in the morning," Darcy promised her friend.

"Kenny already called him," Molly said.

"Good, then tomorrow I'll go out there and see if there's anything I can do to help."

"We'll go out to the stables together," Molly said with determination, her hands tightening into fists.

Darcy knelt down and hugged Molly's slender shoulders. "I'm so sorry, Mol," she said softly.

"We'll get to the bottom of this," Tony assured her. He kissed Darcy's cheek and walked off towards his car.

Darcy turned around to say something to him, but he had disappeared into the darkness.

A strange, empty sensation overcame her, like he was suddenly very distant from her. She shivered in the cold night air, wanting to hear the comforting sound of his voice one last time, but he was gone.

TWELVE

"Scott, we've got to do something!" Darcy yelled into the telephone. She'd dialed his number as soon as she woke up.

"I thought you weren't talking to me anymore," Scott replied tersely.

Darcy tapped her foot on the bottom stair of the Masons' grand staircase, where she was sitting.

"Scott! I'm not kidding," Darcy said.

"Calm down, Darcy," Scott's voice came over the phone. "Just tell me what's up."

"It's about Foxfire and—"

"I know," Scott said. "Kenny called me last night."

"It sounds like a really sick person is doing all this," Darcy said. "What do you think?"

"I'm reserving judgment, but it sounds like that to me, too," Scott said. "Someone with some major-league problems."

"We've got to stop him—or her—now!" said Darcy.

"We?" Scott asked mildly.

"You might not want my help, but you're going to get it," she said with determination.

"Darcy, if you just want to forget about what happened because it's convenient for you now that you want to

96

stick your nose in this, then I'm not interested," he returned evenly.

Darcy didn't respond.

"And I don't want to deal with that boyfriend of yours anymore," Scott added.

"Scott!" Darcy pleaded with him. "I've helped you before."

There was a long silence on the other end of the phone.

"Okay," he said finally. "I'm heading over to the stables in a few minutes. I'll pick you up on the way. But I don't want to hear a word about Tony. See you soon." He hung up.

Scott arrived twenty minutes later. Both Darcy and Molly were downstairs, ready and waiting.

"Hope you don't mind an extra passenger," said Molly, pulling on a sweater.

Scott exchanged looks with Darcy. Darcy just shrugged. She wasn't going to tell Molly she couldn't go.

"Molly, I don't want you hanging around there. It might be dangerous," he said.

Molly spun around in her chair to look at him. "Listen, Scott-the-Cop. My horse could be hurt next. So I'm going and there's nothing you can do about it. If you don't take me along, I'll meet you there."

"Okay, we're wasting time. Let's go," Scott said.

Once they were in Scott's car heading over to Foxfire, Darcy started to talk about the case. "I have a theory," she said. "I think that the person who's doing this knows a lot about horses and riders."

"Why's that?" Scott asked.

"Wait! Stop!" Molly held her hand up and listened to the report coming over Scott's police radio.

"Fire at Foxfire Stables, on Shore Road. Firefighters on way to scene. Additional companies being called in from Portland and Freeport. No casualty reports. All cars in immediate vicinity please report to Foxfire Stables. Repeat . . .

"Oh, God!" Molly moaned, burying her face in her hands. "Oh my God! Ebony will die! Horses hate fire!"

Scott slapped a whirling red bulb onto the roof of his car and snapped on the siren. He raced along Shore Road to the stables. Minutes later they saw flames and smoke reaching into the sky.

"There it is!" Molly screamed. "It looks awful!"

Darcy could see flames leaping out of the side of the barn where the stalls were. People were running around everywhere. Horses in the paddocks ran amok, crazed by the smoke and commotion. The smoke was thick like fog. "Oh, my horse—oh, no, Ebony!" screamed Molly at the top of her lungs.

The car screeched to a halt in front of the barn and Molly pushed at Scott to get out of the car.

"Get Ebony out of there—no matter what else you do—just get him out!" Molly cried.

"We'll try," Darcy promised, as she and Scott sprinted towards the burning barn.

Suddenly Scott grabbed Darcy's sleeve. "Look—what's that?"

Darcy squinted at the barn. Emerging from the smoke and flames was a horse.

"Ebony!" screamed Darcy, racing towards the horse.

"Who's that with him?" asked Scott. "There's someone clinging to his mane!"

Darcy looked at the form and suddenly gasped. "It's Kenny. How'd he do that?"

As they drew closer, Darcy heard Kenny's soft, low voice as he crooned to Ebony: "There boy, good horse, what a good horse, it's okay now, we're safe."

Just then, a huge crack echoed behind them. Darcy and Scott looked up and saw the back part of the barn, where Kenny had just come from, cave in from the top and collapse in flames.

Ebony lunged forward at the sound, and Kenny flew off of him.

"Get him! Grab the halter and hold him!" Scott ordered Darcy, pushing her towards the horse. "I'll keep him away from Kenny!"

Darcy raced towards the horse and grabbed the halter. Ebony raised his head high in the air, taking Darcy's arm with it. Without thinking, Darcy yanked him down, and started leading him towards the car and Molly. Only when she got near the car did she realize that she was trembling all over with fear.

Darcy tied Ebony to a hitching post near the car and raced back to Kenny, who was lying in a heap on the ground. Scott was nowhere to be found.

"Where's Scott? Did you see him?" asked Darcy.

"No—oh, God, he's not in there is he?" Kenny pleaded.

"I don't know!" Darcy yelled. Then Kenny started hacking uncontrollably because of all the smoke he'd taken in. Darcy tried to comfort him. Then she stood and ran towards the barn shouting, "Scott! Scott!"

I can't let anything happen to him, she thought wildly. *I have to find him—I have to!*

Suddenly, off to her left, Darcy saw Ina run in the direction of the barn, jump over some burning debris, and disappear inside.

THIRTEEN

Darcy dug a bandanna out of her pocket and dunked it in a horse's water trough, then held it over her mouth and nose as she entered the burning barn. Flames were shooting everywhere. Faintly, she heard the first fire engine sirens and someone calling her back. She continued.

Okay, I know somehow that there's more cool air down by the ground, Darcy thought to herself.

"Scott!" she shouted, as she dropped to the ground and started to crawl along. "Ouch!" she yelped, as a burning ember hit her in the forehead.

The smoke was so thick she couldn't imagine how Scott could do much of anything in there. Darcy continued to push through the barn, looking for shapes of people or horses. *Where's Scott? Where's Ina?* Darcy couldn't see a thing.

She crawled past the burning ramp for disabled riders. She pushed her way farther into the barn, and then actually saw the top of Scott's head over a stall door. He was with a horse.

"Scott!" she choked out, coughing from the effort.

He turned and saw her. Darcy crawled over and found him struggling to save a chestnut horse. She quickly took the rag away from her nose and held it over the horse's nose, as she and Scott looked for a safe route out.

Suddenly, a huge pile of hay in the stall burst into flames. The horse panicked and started running. It was all Darcy and Scott could do to follow.

Miraculously, the horse led them out of the barn. As they made their way out, a huge stream of water from one of the fire trucks hit the barn.

"We're out!" Darcy yelled.

"Yes!" yelled Scott.

"You guys okay?" asked a rescue-suited fireman. Darcy and Scott nodded.

"Good," the fireman said. "Now stay clear of the barn!"

Darcy made her way back to Scott's car to check on Molly. There were two rescue workers standing there, talking on Scott's radio.

"Anyone else in there?" one of them asked Darcy.

"I don't think so—wait! There's Ina! I saw her run into the barn!" Darcy remembered.

"We'll check it out," one of them told her.

Darcy turned her attention to Molly, who one of the rescue workers had taken out of Scott's car and set in her wheelchair. Molly had wheeled herself over to Ebony, who was nuzzling her.

"You're a hero," Molly said simply, when Darcy approached. "Scott, too."

"Thanks," Darcy said. "So is Kenny. I'm glad Ebony got out." Just then Scott came over and joined them. Molly thanked him, too.

"Where'd you learn that bandanna trick?" Scott asked Darcy. "I couldn't have done it without you."

"Oh, probably just something I saw on TV," she said.

"Let go of me!" a voice cried.

Darcy and Scott looked over and saw Tony bringing a struggling Ina over to them.

Something seems out of place, thought Darcy. *Where has he been during all this?*

"What's going on?" asked Darcy.

Tony stopped in front of her and Scott, with Ina still trying to pull away from him. "I caught her running down that side road with the petty cash box," he said breathlessly. "She's been stealing the money."

Ina's gaze was wild. "I didn't do it," she said.

"That's not all!" Tony said. "Check out what's in her pockets. Matches!"

"Maybe she smokes. Do you smoke, Ina?" asked Scott.

"She doesn't. Just one match to that stack of hay could've lit the whole place up," said Tony.

Darcy sensed something wasn't right—*I've seen her with cigarettes, I think,* she thought, *but I can't exactly remember when. And Tony's the one who keeps telling me she wouldn't hurt a flea!*

"I didn't do it," mumbled Ina, staring at Scott.

"Ina, you're under arrest for larceny," Scott said. "Do you know anything about how this fire started?" he asked gently.

"I said I didn't do it. Doesn't anyone hear me?" she cried shrilly.

Scott bundled Ina safely into the backseat of the car. He turned to Tony. "How did you find her?"

"Running from the scene," said Tony. "Clutching the cash box."

"I don't think she's a hardened criminal, but I want to thank you," said Scott, extending his hand to Tony.

Tony looked surprised. *He looks how I feel,* thought Darcy, watching this.

"And I'm sorry for what I said before, treating you like a criminal," said Scott.

Wow, shocker number two, thought Darcy. *I never thought I'd hear that in this century.*

"Hey, it's okay, man," said Tony, smiling at him. "I've got a big mess to clean up here," he continued, surveying the smoking remains. "I just hope the horses are all okay."

Firemen still strode around with hoses and other equipment, making sure every spark was dead. Scott went over to the fire chief and talked to him for a while, then came back with some news.

"He says that none of the horses look injured and nobody's hurt," said Scott. "But I'm pretty sure somebody did this on purpose."

"Why do you think that?" Molly piped up.

"Just a feeling," Scott said. "A pattern, maybe." As he spoke, one of the rescue unit people wheeled Kenny over on a spare wheelchair they kept in their truck. Kenny was dirty and his hair was singed, but he didn't seem to care about anything but the horses.

"We need to trailer the horses to Sunset Stables until we can get things straight around here," he said.

"Good idea," Tony said. Molly nodded in agreement.

"One last thing," Scott said, "before I bring Ina to the station. Kenny, how did you get Molly's horse out of that barn. You're the real hero here."

Darcy saw Molly look at Kenny with admiration.

"Well," Kenny said, "I was sort of up on the mounting ramp when the fire broke out. I tried to lead Ebony out then, but he wouldn't budge. So I grabbed him around the neck and he really hauled out."

"Wow," said Molly.

"I'm really amazed," Scott said. "I'll make sure the newspaper reporters know about this."

Darcy watched as Scott slid into the front seat and radioed headquarters that he was bringing Ina in. Ina was curled up in the backseat like a forlorn child. Darcy looked in at her scared, confused face.

She has to be the one who set the fire, thought Darcy. *This is one messed-up girl!* But somehow, Darcy had a feeling that Ina wasn't the end of the story. *And if it wasn't Ina who did this, who could it be?* Then Darcy dismissed the feeling from her mind. *I've been wrong before, she thought, and I'm probably wrong now.*

FOURTEEN

"Darcy—mail for you!" Caroline Mason called up the stairs later that night. "I forgot to tell you before. Looks like an interesting envelope," she added when Darcy appeared on the landing.

Darcy hurried down the stairs, noting the wild, slinky black pajama suit Mrs. Mason wore. Her hair was piled up on the top of her head and speared with what looked like two human bones.

"Who'd you knock off to get the bone barrettes?" Darcy teased, pointing to Caroline's hair.

"Just a few of Gomez's more tiresome relatives," Caroline said, fluffing her hair around the ornaments.

"I always say, relatives make the best jewelry," Darcy said, looking over the envelope package. "Hey, it's from the *Washington Post!*"

"What is it?" asked Caroline curiously.

"I sent away for some of Tony's articles to surprise him for his birthday," Darcy said. "Thanks," she added, and bounded up the stairs to her room. She tore open the envelope, thinking how psyched Tony would be when she gave him the surprise scrapbook.

There was a letter on top—from the editor:

Dear Ms. Laken:

Thank you for your inquiry about one of our authors. Unfortunately, we have no record of an "Antonio Mendez" ever writing for the Post. I did look in the files to see if perhaps we had a file on him, because the name sounded familiar. Two articles about Antonio Mendez are enclosed. We have no way of knowing, of course, if this is the person you are referring to.

Again, thanks for your interest and good luck!

Weird, Darcy thought. Slowly, she pushed the cover letter aside to reveal the first clip. Her heart nearly stopped. She stared at a newsprint photo of a little five-year-old boy with dark hair and haunted eyes. And then she closed her own eyes, as a fear so chilling she could barely breathe crawled over her skin. She knew before she even looked at the date on the article that it would be very old. She recognized those haunted eyes in the photo. They belonged to Tony.

Almost against her will, she read the story entitled, "Boy Found Tied in Burning Barn":

Five-year-old Antonio Mendez was found Saturday tied to a post in a Maryland barn that had caught fire while his parents, Roberto and Delia Mendez, were out riding. Officials are not certain as to what caused the blaze. Social workers had previously visited the home because of recurring reports of child abuse, but no clear evidence was found. The child is now in satisfactory condition at Valley Memorial, after being treated for smoke inhalation, dehydration, and malnutrition.

"Tony," Darcy whispered, tears quickly filling her eyes. She tried to imagine the unbearable pain of this poor child. *My God, it's almost too horrible to comprehend, and yet Tony lived through it.* With shaking hands she looked at the next clipping, a small one, dated two years ago:

> *A fire that broke out at a Virginia stable today claimed the lives of ten horses. Fire chief Frank Boley said fire fighters were still investigating the cause of the blaze, but arson was a distinct possibility. Held for questioning was twenty-year-old Antonio Mendez, a riding instructor at the stable, who was ultimately released because of insufficient evidence.*

"Please don't let this be true," Darcy whispered out loud, but even as she made the plea, the sinking feeling in her heart told her it was hopeless. She bit her lower lip and tried to stop her hands from shaking. Who was the Tony she was so crazy about? Had everything he told her been a lie? Was he deeply and seriously sick?

"No! I don't believe that!" Darcy cried, jumping off her bed. She picked up the papers and ran into Molly's room.

"What?" Molly asked, putting down the book she was reading. "You look like a ghost."

"It's, it's . . ." Darcy hardly knew where to begin.

"Oh, no, did something happen at Sunset Stables?" Molly cried.

"No, nothing like that," Darcy said quickly. She sat down next to Molly on the bed and wordlessly handed her the letter and the clippings. "Read this."

Molly read the letter first, then scanned the clips. "This is unbelievable!" Molly breathed.

"I . . . I just don't know how to . . ." Darcy's voice trailed off, and silent tears fell down her cheeks. "Molly, everything Tony told me must be a lie! He didn't travel through Europe. His mother isn't a diplomat!"

"Darcy," Molly said sympathetically, putting her hand over Darcy's.

"He's sick, Molly, really sick. And I must be sick, too, because I fell in love with a phantom who doesn't really exist!"

Molly gulped hard. "You think he did all those awful things? How could he? He passed the lie detector test! You were there yourself!"

Then Darcy remembered something that Professor Aaron had said: *"Polygraph tests are useful, but they are not infallible. A sociopath personality who cannot tell right from wrong will often fool the examiner."* And Tony had even made a point of telling her himself that the test wasn't foolproof.

Darcy forced back her tears and set her jaw hard.

"They're not perfect, Molly! Omigod, I had a dream. A voice was begging me—'Stop me,' it kept saying."

"Tony!" Molly gasped.

"And I didn't stop him!" Darcy cried. "I didn't want to believe it was him! I thought it was Ina!"

"You can't blame yourself—" Molly interrupted.

"I can't?" Darcy shot back. "God, I hate myself for this! What good is it to know things when the people I love get hurt anyway?"

Molly stared silently at her friend. "I don't blame you for what happened to me," she finally said.

"But Molly, I blame me," Darcy sobbed. "I blame me!"

Molly put her arms around Darcy and held her until Darcy managed to stop sobbing.

"Okay," Darcy said, blowing her nose with a tissue from Molly's vanity table. "I can't run away from this. I have to call Scott and tell him."

"Use my phone," Molly urged.

Molly read through the clips one more time while Darcy called Scott. The phone rang and rang, and Darcy closed her eyes and prayed. *Oh, please, Scott, be there. . . .*

"Yeah?" Scott finally answered groggily.

"Scott, it's me," Darcy said quickly. "I'm sorry I woke you, but it's important."

"What's up?" Scott asked, instantly alert.

"Look, I know you tried to warn me about Tony. . . ." Darcy began hesitantly.

"Did he hurt you?" Scott asked, his voice steely. "Because I will kill the son of a—"

"No, no, he didn't hurt me," Darcy insisted. "But . . . but you were right about him."

"He did it—all of it—didn't he," Scott said in a flat voice.

"I think so," Darcy admitted. "It's too complicated to explain on the phone. Will you go over to Sunset Stables with us? We've got to go check on the horses, and we've got to get to Tony before he hurts someone else."

"I'm on my way," Scott said, and hung up quickly.

Darcy helped Molly dress and they waited downstairs for Scott's car to drive up.

"The horses are back at Sunset Stables now," Molly told Scott as Darcy helped her into the car. "We've got to go check on Ebony and the other horses."

"You explain; I'll drive," Scott told Darcy as he headed his car down the private drive.

Darcy forced herself to tell Scott everything, not stopping until he knew the entire story. "So, that's it," she finished. "I guess you were right about him all along."

"Whoa," Scott exhaled, shaking his head. "That's some story." He looked over at Darcy. "I'm glad you're okay," he added in a low voice.

"I don't believe Tony would ever hurt me," Darcy said fervently.

Scott grimaced. "An hour ago you wouldn't have believed any of this other stuff about him, either."

"I know," Darcy admitted, her voice hushed. Guilty tears sprang to her eyes. "How could I have been so wrong?"

FIFTEEN

Scott hustled over to Sunset Stables. It was a well-known place on the island. They pulled into the parking lot and Darcy watched as Scott flipped on the dome light of the cruiser. A man came quickly to the door of the main house wearing a robe. Scott got out of the car to go talk to him, and Darcy and Molly followed, after Darcy got Molly set up in her wheelchair.

"Isn't it a little late to be calling?" asked the man.

"Sorry about this. Officer Scott Phillips, Sunset Island Police," Scott said, flashing his badge.

The man looked at Darcy and Molly. "And you two are you policewomen?"

"No, this is really important, though," Darcy burst out.

"What seems to be the trouble?" the man asked.

"Are you one of the Berensons?" Scott asked, mentioning the name of the family that ran the stables. "You don't look familiar."

"Was the last time I checked," said the man. "I've been away for the last year or so. I'm the brother of the owner. Come in out of the cold." He opened the door wide.

"We aren't here for a social call," said Darcy. "We're worried about the horses you took in for Foxfire Stables."

"As far as I know, they're fine," said Mr. Berenson.

"Can we take a look at them and just make sure nothing's happened in the night?" asked Scott. "We're following a lead."

Mr. Berenson frowned. "This sounds serious. You can't tell me what it's about?"

"Only that the horses might be in danger, sir," said Molly.

"A-yuh, let me get my flashlight," said Mr. Berenson. "Wait here." He was back in seconds with a big industrial flashlight.

"What are we waiting for?" Mr. Berenson asked. "Let's go." He led the way out to his main paddock, Darcy pushing Molly along in the darkness.

"Have you noticed any problems with the horses lately?" asked Scott as they walked across the yard to the stables.

"Nope, they're fine," said Mr. Berenson. He glanced at Molly. "Why do you want to be out on a cold night like this?"

"Because my horse, Ebony, is staying here," explained Molly.

"Oh, I know him—he's in that far stall. You must be the girl who had that accident. I heard about you. It's a shame."

Darcy wheeled Molly over to Ebony to take at look at him. He looked fine. They went back to join Mr. Berenson and Scott.

"Have you seen anybody hanging around the place lately?" asked Darcy fearfully. *God, let him say no.*

"Nope, I haven't seen anyone," Mr. Berenson said. He glanced again at his watch, but opened the barn door so they could go inside.

In the stable, the warm scents of hay and horse manure mingled as Mr. Berenson turned on a light. Horses stirred, and some whinnied in greeting. Darcy and Scott walked along, looking in every stall, but there was nothing out of the ordinary.

"Looks fine to me, and I think I'd know if anything was amiss," said Mr. Berenson. "What do you think, young man?"

"Looks fine," Scott admitted. "Anything strange happens, call us, okay? We'll come out, day or night."

"I have no doubt of that, sonny," Mr. Berenson said, grinning at him.

Next stop was Foxfire, or what was left of Foxfire. As they pulled in, they could see a few cars in the parking lot.

"Tony's Toyota is here. Good," said Scott, surveying the dark lot.

"Okay, we're going to need Kenny," said Darcy.

Scott looked at her. "Darcy, you and Molly stay here."

"No way are we staying here," piped Molly as she looked out at the parking lot. "We stay together."

"I'm running this show, guys," Scott said. "This isn't a joke."

Suddenly, they heard a tapping on the glass of the police car. They all whirled towards the sound. It was Kenny, bundled in an overcoat, sitting in his wheelchair with a big grin on his face.

"Heckuva time for a visit," he said, "but we're friendly types here. What's up guys? I heard you pull in."

"We have to talk, Kenny," said Scott. "Can we all go inside for a while?"

Kenny nodded, and when they were out of the car he led the way into the den of the old farmhouse. Kenny snapped on some lights, they all sat down, and Darcy wasted no time in handing Kenny the letter from the *Washington Post* and the clips.

As he read, his face paled. "I never would've thought this of Tony."

"We've got to find him now!" Molly whispered loudly.

"Which room is his?" Scott asked, standing up. "I'll take you there," said Kenny. "Lemme warn you—the guy sleeps like a log."

He whirled his chair around and started down the hall. Then he knocked on Tony's door. There was no answer.

"See what I mean?" said Kenny.

Darcy realized she had never seen Tony's room before.

"Tony! Wake up! It's Kenny!" Kenny said into the door. Still no answer.

Kenny tried the doorknob and it opened. He pushed the door open wide. No Tony.

Darcy, Molly, Scott and Kenny moved into the room and looked around. The bed was neatly made, there was a stack of receipts held down by a large rock on one corner of the dresser. All Tony's clothes were hung in the closet. A couple of books sat on the nightstand. *Where is he?* Darcy thought. *Why isn't he here?*

Scott moved around the room, looking at everything with an expert eye. Running his finger along the dresser, he held up a clean finger. "No dust. It's kind of like he cleaned up before leaving."

"Leaving?" Darcy said in alarm. *He would just leave without telling me? But look what else he didn't tell me—you haven't really known him all this time; you've known a myth!* "But his car is still here!"

Scott turned to Kenny. "Did he pay his rent on time?"

"Yes, he did, and—"

A sudden flash of white light moved across Darcy's consciousness. She took a step backward, felt slightly dizzy, then recovered a second later.

"Darcy? Are you okay?" Molly asked.

Scott stared into her face, and then he was holding her by the shoulders. "You looked like you were going to keel over for a minute there."

"I just thought of something, or didn't think . . . I don't know," she stammered. "I think we really need to search for him. He's in trouble. Maybe in the barn."

"There aren't any horses in the barn now," Kenny reminded her.

"That doesn't matter!" said Molly impatiently. "Okay, let's go," said Kenny, "but let's check here first." Scott led the way and they looked in every room of the house. Nothing.

"Okay," Scott said, "We'll go look in the barn. But be careful." He pulled out his police-issue flashlight, and Kenny grabbed one of his own. Soon, two wide beams of light cut a path through the darkness on the way to the barn.

"There're no lights in what's left of the barn," said Kenny. "Gone with the fire."

Darcy wheeled Molly into the burnt-out barn, staying close to Scott and Kenny. It smelled awful. *It could come crashing down on us at any minute,* she thought.

Scott and Kenny trained the flashlights on the blackened interior of the barn.

"Man, it's spooky in here," said Molly, wheeling along on the charred straw.

Kenny chuckled softly. "That's something—coming from you."

"Tony? Tony . . . are you in here?" Darcy called, but all she could hear was the steady grinding sound of a weather-vane turning on the roof, the crunch of two sets of wheels on the barn floor and an occasional creak.

"Yo . . . Tony!" called Scott. His voice echoed eerily in the dark barn.

"What's that weird sound?" asked Molly. "That creaking."

"Just the remains of the barn settling," said Kenny as he moved off to the left to peer into the blackened stalls. They were careful not to get too close to the collapsed area of stalls.

Darcy wheeled Molly into the end of the barn where the mounting ramp had been. Now it was a pile of collapsed blackened lumber, and in the half-light of the flashlights, it looked like a giant blackbird with its wings outstretched.

"What's that?" asked Molly.

"That used to be the mounting ramp," said Darcy.

Suddenly one of the flashlights shone on something up ahead. Molly let out a bloodcurdling scream and stiffened in her chair.

A split second later, Darcy saw what Molly saw and gripped the handles of the wheelchair for dear life—afraid that if she let go, she would faint dead away.

The flashlight rested on something—somebody—hanging by a rope from the rafters. Darcy moved a little closer, her heart pounding so loud she could hear nothing else. Then it was painfully clear: a limp human form, its head cocked to one side at an odd, unnatural angle, black hair untidily flung across its forehead. The creaking sound of the rope as it swung slightly back and forth, back and forth, now seemed to cut through the night air.

"Noooooooo!" Molly's piercing scream shook Darcy from her stupor.

In that instant, Darcy lifted her gaze and met Tony's—his lifeless eyes seemed to stare right into her own.

SIXTEEN

"Darcy."

Darcy heard her name and felt a pair of firm hands on her shoulders. She didn't know until that moment that she was trembling throughout her entire body.

"I'm here, Darcy."

She knew that the voice and touch belonged to Scott. For what seemed like an eternity, she was frozen in place, her fingers gripping Molly's wheelchair, her eyes fixed on Tony's body. She stared at it, expecting it to suddenly come to life, expecting that maybe this was all some kind of awful nightmare. Kenny drew up to Molly's side and took her hand, and Darcy heard Molly's sobbing and reached out a hand to stroke her head.

There was nothing anyone could do.

Finally, Darcy moved out from behind the chair and went straight up to the dead body.

"Darcy, don't," Scott said quickly, but she ignored him.

She touched Tony's limp hand and found it cold. "I'm so sorry," she whispered to him. Her gaze traveled down to the ground, near his dangling feet. A crumpled slip of paper lay there as though he had held it in his hand and it had fallen the moment he died.

Kneeling down, Darcy picked up the paper and uncrumpled it. It shook in her trembling fingers. The note read quite simply: "Stop me."

Stop me, please stop me. Oh, God, Darcy cried in her heart. *He was begging me for help, and I ignored it.*

"Darcy, let me have that, please," Scott said softly, holding out his hand to her.

"What?" she said dully.

"The note—let me have it," he said, his face echoing her own pain. "It's evidence."

"Right," Darcy said. She sounded robotic to herself—as if someone had taken over her power of speech. "I guess I shouldn't have touched it without gloves. Now my fingerprints are on it."

"It's okay, Darcy," Scott said, reaching out to touch her arm.

"Now that my fingerprints are on the note, I could be a suspect," Darcy continued in the same flat voice. "I should be a suspect, really, because I'm guilty."

"It's not your fault!" Molly managed to gulp out between her sobs.

"Darcy, please," Scott said, gently touching her face. But it was as if she didn't feel a thing, as if nothing could reach her.

"Everyone out of the barn," Scott finally ordered. He turned Darcy around and led her out into the night. Molly and Kenny wheeled themselves out.

"I should have helped him," Darcy whispered, staring into the distance. "He called to me and I turned away. . . ."

Molly wheeled herself in front of Darcy and stared up into the tall girl's face. "Darcy," she said sharply. "You didn't know. You can blame yourself if you want to be some kind of martyr, but it's dumb. You can't be responsible for everyone else's life! Not even mine!"

Something in the sharp tone of Molly's voice penetrated Darcy's fog. Her eyes focused on Molly.

"All you can do is grieve," Molly told her gently. "And then you just have to get on with it. I should know."

"I . . . I . . ." Darcy began. And then the tears began to fall down her cheeks, a cry wrenched from somewhere deep within her, and the next thing she knew, she was sobbing in Scott's arms.

After what seemed like an eternity, the foursome went to Scott's car where he radioed for help.

"This is still so hard to believe," Kenny said. "I mean, Tony seemed like such a great guy. Everyone liked him."

"Sociopaths are often really charming," Scott said grimly. "They fool everyone—they're the best liars in the world, because they don't feel guilty when they lie and they don't censor their impulses—no sense of right or wrong."

"But Tony did have a sense of right and wrong," Darcy said passionately. "He wanted to stop, but he couldn't. So he stopped himself the only way he could."

"Poor, messed-up guy," Kenny murmured.

A while later, two police cars and an ambulance pulled into the stable yard. Molly, Darcy and Kenny stayed in the house while Scott dealt with the authorities.

After they had surveyed the scene, Scott brought two policemen into the house.

"Sorry, but they need to interview the three of you for their report," Scott told them.

"Can't you tell them everything they need to know?" asked Molly, looking pale and exhausted.

"No," Scott said gently. "You'll all need to make a statement."

Darcy, Molly and Kenny answered the policemen's questions dutifully. Why had they come to the stables? Who found Tony? What did they see? Had any of them touched the body?

Such dry, impersonal questions, Darcy thought. *Tony was alive, and now he's dead. He died all alone, scared, just like the little boy in the newspaper clipping.*

"Is there any next of kin that you know of?" asked one policeman.

"Both of his parents are dead, I think," said Darcy. "But then he told me so many things that aren't true . . ."

Kenny nodded. "He told me the same stories he told Darcy—that his mom was a British diplomat—stuff like that," Kenny said. "So who knows?"

Finally, the questioning was over and the policemen filed out of the room with Scott.

"Even now, it doesn't seem real," Darcy murmured. "I knew him. . . . I thought I knew him," she amended sadly.

"I guess none of us knew him," Kenny said.

"It's a curse, you know," Darcy said sadly, "having these dreams, knowing things but not knowing what they mean. . . ."

"To be given only enough to be afraid, but not to know what exactly is going on, what will happen," Kenny mused.

"That's it," Darcy agreed softly. "Sometimes it's a terrible curse."

Darcy walked out onto the front porch and stared up at the starlit sky. She closed her eyes and saw Tony's smile, heard his hearty laughter, and felt his lips on hers. *How could someone so full of life be dead?* She stared up at the infinite sky again, searching for answers.

"Oh, Tony," Darcy whispered, "Where are you now? Can you see me?" Tears swam before her eyes, blurring her vision until she caught sight of a shooting star soaring across the sky.

Her father had told her when she was a little girl that you could wish on a shooting star, and the leprechauns would make the wish come true. And so Darcy closed her tear-filled eyes and made her wish: *Tony, wherever you are, I hope you don't hurt anymore.*

SEVENTEEN

"Those jeans are falling off you," Molly told Darcy as Darcy looped a belt through her pants. It was two days after Tony's suicide, and Darcy hadn't much felt like eating.

"There were always kind of baggy," Darcy said. "Which shoes do you want?" she asked, standing in front of Molly's closet.

"The black flats," Molly said, "and you know I can get them myself."

"I know," Darcy said, bringing the shoes to Molly. "I need to keep busy."

"Molly, dear," Caroline Mason called from Molly's open doorway, "a letter came for you."

"Who from?" Molly asked. Caroline handed Molly the letter. "It's from Howie," she said, scanning the return address and tearing open the envelope. Her eyes quickly skimmed the letter, and then she looked up at Darcy and her mother. "You don't have to stare at me like I just won the lottery. It's just a note from a guy."

"How tasteless of me," Caroline said. She kissed her daughter on the forehead and left the room.

"You're not getting rid of me so easily," Darcy said, sitting on Molly's bed. "I want to know what Howie had to say."

"Well, actually, his family is planning to use their summer house on the island for Thanksgiving," Molly said. "He wanted to know if I'll be around."

"That's great, Mol," Darcy said.

"He even invited me for Thanksgiving dinner," Molly added casually.

"No kidding?" Darcy asked. "Are you gonna go?"

"Nah. My parents' Thanksgiving feasts are legendary. They usually invite a dozen or so of their more wacko horror movie friends. Once they served a turkey raw just for effect."

"Sounds ghoulish," Darcy said with a smile.

"I'm glad Howie wrote to me, though," Molly added, staring almost shyly at the letter. "I thought maybe he'd forget all about me once he got back to school. . . ."

"Why would he do that?" Darcy asked. "He's crazy about you!"

"Why is because I am not exactly normal girlfriend material," Molly pointed out.

"That's true," Darcy said honestly. "It'll take an extraordinary guy to really appreciate you. And that guy will be very, very lucky, because you are so incredibly cool."

Molly laughed. "You are so full of it."

The phone rang by Molly's bed. Darcy picked it up.

"Hello?"

"Hi, it's Kenny."

"Oh, hi," Darcy said, the warmth in her voice obvious.

"I wanted to let you and Molly know, Tony's funeral is the day after tomorrow at ten-thirty, at the Episcopal Church on the bay side."

"Did you arrange it?" Darcy asked.

"I would have, but it turns out Tony has a next-of-kin after all. There was a name and address in his wallet. She told me she's his aunt—that's really all I know."

"Thanks for letting us know," Darcy told him.

"Sure," said Kenny. "See you then."

Darcy hung up and told Molly exactly what Kenny had just told her.

"An aunt?" Molly repeated with surprise.

"That's what Kenny said." Darcy shook her head. "Did I ever really know him at all?" she asked Molly.

"I don't know," Molly replied.

"He was so sophisticated, so exciting . . ." Darcy mused, "but that person was just an illusion."

"So, I wonder," Molly asked, "does that mean you weren't really in love?"

Darcy shrugged. "My dad always told me that real love is something that grows sweeter with time, like wine."

"Yuck!" Molly said. "Seriously hokey!"

"I guess," Darcy agreed with a sad smile. "Hey, speaking of love, remember when you told me you'd never know what it would be like to have two cute guys panting after you? Well, you can now officially eat those words."

Molly flushed. "You mean Howie and Kenny?"

"Exactly."

"I like both of them," Molly admitted.

"Well, then, see both of them," Darcy said firmly, "as long as you tell them the truth about each other."

"I guess you learned that the hard way," Molly said.

"Right," Darcy agreed.

"Well, there's a benefit concert at Foxfire next week to help raise money to rebuild from the fire," Molly said.

"Flirting with Danger is playing. Kenny already invited me. So I'll tell him about Howie then."

"Smart move," Darcy approved.

"Kenny says they're planning to expand the riding program, too. And they need to hire someone to replace Tony."

Darcy winced at this news. It seemed impossible that Tony had caused all this devastation, and now, just a few days after his death, efforts were being made to repair Foxfire. And to hire a new horse trainer—someone was sure to be hired to give riding lessons in Tony's place. People filled in when other people left, filled in the empty space as quickly as possible. Darcy wondered if anyone but Molly, Kenny, Scott and herself would remember Tony a year from now.

* * *

"Look, a woman is sitting in the family section," Molly whispered to Darcy. It was two days later, and they had just taken seats in a middle pew for Tony's funeral service. Scott, Kenny and Ina sat next to them. The only other people there were Kenny's parents, Professor Aaron from their criminology course, and a couple of other people that Darcy thought she'd seen around school. The casket was closed.

Darcy craned her neck and saw a woman's head, wrapped in a black veil, bowed in prayer. *The mysterious aunt,* Darcy thought to herself. She knew that this woman might be the only one who could shed some light on who Tony really was, something she desperately wanted to know. It was as if she couldn't make peace with herself until she knew.

The service began. Once again, Darcy found herself praying that Tony, at last, had found some kind of peace. All her life the church had taught her that suicide was a sin, but nothing seemed that simple. *Dear God,* Darcy prayed, *I don't have any answers. But please, take care of the hurt little boy that Tony really was.*

The woman in the black veil sobbed as the minister gave a short speech about Tony's sad and untimely death. Darcy felt the tears coming again and squashed them back down. She pressed her hands together in her lap, then smoothed a crease out of the black dress she had borrowed from Molly's mother.

Organ notes filled the sanctuary as the last hymn sounded. Darcy stood up and Scott held the hymn book because her hands were shaking. She started to sing but her voice cracked and she couldn't get the words out. Scott slipped his arm around her shoulders and he sang in a gentle tenor.

Finally, it was over. Tony's lone relative walked down the aisle with her head bowed. Darcy filed out with her friends and looked for the woman once they were outside.

Suddenly, Ina grabbed Darcy's sleeve and stared at her with her pale blue eyes. "I'm so sorry about Tony. I didn't know he was unhappy."

"Neither did I, Ina," said Darcy, swallowing hard.

Ina still had hold of Darcy's sleeve. "I love the horses more than people, so I don't notice stuff with people. I wish I'd noticed about Tony, though."

Darcy nodded. She was too choked up to speak.

"I'm sorry Tony's dead," Ina added, staring at the ground. "And I'm sorry I stole the money. But I didn't take it from the fire that time. I was just afraid there were horses still in the barn."

Darcy put her hand on Ina's arm. "Thanks," she said quietly. "I was awfully hard on you, and I'm sorry about that."

"Ina," Scott said, "if you promise to pay back the money and stop stealing, I'll help you get your job back."

"No kidding?" Ina's eyes widened with excitement. "I love my job."

"Excuse me," Darcy said. She saw the woman in the black veil standing by herself, looking through her purse. Darcy walked over to her.

The woman turned around and lifted her veil. She looked about forty-five, with light brown hair framing her soft, round face. There was something in her dark brown eyes that reminded Darcy of Tony.

"I don't mean to intrude . . ." Darcy said to the woman, "but I was wondering if I could speak with you for a moment."

Darcy took a deep breath. "I'm Darcy Laken. I was . . . a friend of Tony's."

"I'm Linda Pawling, his aunt," the woman said.

"Tony and I . . ." Darcy began, trying to explain their relationship. But what was it really? Had she been Tony's girlfriend? How could that be true, when she never really knew him at all? "We were seeing each other," she finally said.

"I didn't even know he was in Maine," Linda said with a sigh. "He didn't stay in touch."

"I know about his childhood," Darcy blurted out. "I mean, I know about what was in the paper." She told Linda exactly what had been sent to her from the *Washington Post*.

"Poor little boy," Linda said. "Poor, poor little boy. His mother—my sister—was a battered woman, as well as being a drug addict. She couldn't stand up to that bastard she married."

"Couldn't you get Tony some help?" Darcy asked plaintively.

"Don't you think I tried?" Linda burst out. "He lived with me for a few years after his parents deserted him. But he was such a troubled child—setting fires, killing his own pet bunny. What was I supposed to do? I couldn't handle him!"

"So where did he go?" Darcy asked fearfully.

"I found him a very good private center," Linda said defensively. "I always saw that he was well taken care of financially."

"How long did he live at this center?" Darcy asked.

"Until he was eighteen," Linda said. "He received therapy there. They said he was cured—"

"Cured?" Darcy echoed. "How could they have said he was cured?"

"Young lady, I'm not a psychiatrist," Linda said, her bottom lip quivering. "I did the best I could, which is more than my sister deserved, quite frankly."

It was everything Darcy could do not to pick the woman up and shake her until her teeth rattled out of her head. "We're not talking about your sister," Darcy said, gritting her teeth. "We're talking about your nephew. Where did he go after they released him?"

"I wouldn't know. He didn't choose to contact me, even though I set him up with a fund that would take care of all his financial needs for life," Linda said indignantly. "I guess he never really cared about me." Tears welled up in Linda's eyes—tears of self-pity. Darcy stared at her, thinking she'd never in her life loathed a person as much as she now loathed Tony's aunt.

"Thank you for your time," Darcy said, and abruptly turned away from the woman. She felt as if she were going to be sick.

"What's the aunt like?" Scott asked when Darcy walked back over to him.

"Awful," Darcy said. "I don't want to talk about it." Darcy's hands were trembling with anger.

"Want to go for a walk?" Scott asked gently.

Darcy nodded. Molly was near the car talking with Kenny. She walked over and told Molly she'd be back shortly. Then she and Scott walked slowly towards a small wooded area.

"I never knew anyone who died before," Darcy finally said. "Not someone young, I mean."

"Yeah, we all think we're immortal," Scott said ironically. "Being a cop cures you of that notion really fast."

Darcy turned to look at him. Thin sunlight streamed through the pine branches and caught the highlights in his blond hair.

"Scott, I'm so sorry."

He stared at her.

"I . . . I hurt you, and I didn't mean to," Darcy said earnestly. "I just . . . just . . ."

"Just screwed up?" Scott suggested.

"Yeah," Darcy admitted.

"Look, we never said we weren't going to see other people," Scott said. "But you should have just told me you wanted to."

"I didn't want to, until I met Tony!" Darcy exclaimed.

"Or who you thought was Tony," Scott pointed out.

"Right," Darcy agreed sadly. She gave a short, bitter laugh. "I'm so full of it. I always thought I'd be the last girl to fall for some fantasy."

"Hey, you're human," Scott said with a shrug.

"Are you going to be able to forgive me?" she asked him.

Scott stared up at a small patch of sky through the trees. "That impetuous side of you gets you in trouble, you know."

"I know," Darcy replied.

"I'm not going to turn into some kind of daredevil just to get you to want to be with me," Scott warned. "I mean, what you see is what you get."

"I know," Darcy said again.

Finally, Scott looked her in the eye. Then he put his arms around her. "You know, Darcy, I've never even kissed you."

"Kiss me now," Darcy said softly.

"Nope," Scott said. "Not here. It doesn't feel right, given the circumstances. But soon."

Darcy sighed. "Scott, we're talking about one kiss."

"Not necessarily," Scott said in a low voice. He gently lifted a strand of hair from Darcy's face. "When I kiss you, I don't necessarily intend to stop."

"Well, then, I'll settle for a hug," Darcy said, reaching to put her arms around Scott's neck.

He held her for a long time, there amongst the trees. Darcy closed her eyes and laid her head against his strong chest. She could hear the steady beating of his heart.

It felt like coming home.

For sales, editorial information, subsidiary rights
information or a catalog, please write or phone or e-mail
SPLASH
Manhanset House
Shelter Island Hts., New York 11965-0342, US
Tel: 212-427-7139
www.ibooksinc.com
bricktower@aol.com
www.IngramContent.com

www.ingramcontent.com/pod-product-compliance
Lightning Source LLC
Chambersburg PA
CBHW070940250626
47159CB00009B/3323